BEACH BLANKET HOMICIDE

MARIA GERACI

INTRODUCTION

Everyone agrees that Lucy McGuffin bakes the best muffins in Whispering Bay, but she's got another talent, one that she's tried her whole life to hide. Lucy can always tell when a person is lying or telling the truth. Being a human lie detector isn't all it's cracked up to be. Especially when you don't really want the answer to the universal question, "Does this dress make my butt look too big?"

When Lucy is hired to cater the grand opening celebration of the city's new community center, she stumbles across the dead body of Abby Delgado, a prominent member of the Sunshine Ghost Society. Lucy's brother, Father Sebastian, a local priest, is the last person to have seen Abby alive. Convinced he'll be breaking a confidence, Sebastian refuses to cooperate with the police, forcing Lucy to put her skills to the test to save her brother's good name.

Enter the town's new hotshot deputy, Travis Fontaine. Travis doesn't want an amateur like Lucy snooping around his turf, so he offers her a deal. He'll stay out of her kitchen if she stays away from his crime scenes. But Lucy isn't about to let her brother's fate rest in the hands of an arrogant cop.

Good thing she has her best friend, Will, and her new rescue dog, Paco, to back her up, because it's up to Lucy to figure out what everyone in the quaint little beachside town is hiding.

CHAPTER ONE

IT IS a truth universally acknowledged that everyone lies.

I don't say this to be judgmental. Lying is part of the human psyche. Even my perfect, older brother Sebastian, a priest and the pastor at St. Perpetua's Catholic Church here in Whispering Bay, resorts to the occasional fib.

"I left the rectory ten minutes ago. The traffic is murder," Sebastian said just the other day when he was late meeting me for dinner.

"You're not even in the car, are you?" I shot back.

Sebastian let out the sort of long-suffering sigh he'd mastered long before he'd thought of becoming a priest. "Cut me some slack, Lucy, I'll be there as soon as I can."

Most people can see through those kinds of lies. Those are the easy ones. The thing is, I can also see through the trickier, more deceptive lies as well, which sounds like a good thing, right?

Not necessarily.

When I was five, a brand-new set of paintbrushes went missing in my kindergarten class. Our teacher, Mrs. Jackson, tore apart our small classroom looking for them. Eventually, she asked us kids if we knew where they were. No one admitted to anything, but there was something odd in Brittany Kelly's demeanor. Some small tell that went unnoticed by everyone. Except me.

After class, I went to Mrs. Jackson and told her that I thought Brittany had taken the brushes.

"How do you know this?" she asked.

My naïve five-year-old self shrugged. "I don't know. I just do."

"Lucille McGuffin," she said, using my full name like she meant business. "It's not nice to accuse someone without proof." She narrowed her eyes at me. "Are you sure you didn't take them?"

A week later, Brittany admitted to taking the brushes.

Now, did Mrs. Jackson ever give me credit for exposing the culprit, or apologize for accusing me? Nope. All I got for my honesty was a letter sent home to my parents telling them that I was a tattletale, and even worse, Brittany Kelly as a lifelong enemy (and believe me, over the years she's made me suffer).

By high school, I'd pretty much concluded that despite what people said, no one really wanted to know if their boyfriend was cheating on them or if the real reason they'd been excluded from the math club was because they had bad breath.

How I was chosen to receive this "gift" is a mystery. If

someone up there wanted to give me special powers, why couldn't I have been born with the ability to pick winning lottery numbers? Or a perfect nose? I'd kill for a cute little button nose. Or better yet, a metabolism that allows me to eat all the muffins I want without gaining weight.

Lies are a daily occurrence in everyone's life, and I just have to live with them as best I can, which for me, means to smile and ignore them.

Take right now. I'm currently being lied to by Abby Delgado.

"Lucy, you know I didn't order this." She looks with disgust at the sandwich I've just delivered to her table. "When have you known me to like tuna?"

Abby is kind of a character. She's a member of the Sunshine Ghost Society, an organization that communes with the dead. Or so they say. She's a regular customer here at The Bistro by the Beach, the café I co-own along with my friend, Sarah Powers.

Sarah and I are the perfect team. She makes incredible comfort food and I make the best muffins in town, which might sound like I'm bragging, but everyone says so, so who am I to question them?

A couple of weeks ago I sent an audition tape to the Cooking Channel for a chance to appear on *Muffin Wars*. Think *Cupcake Wars*, but with muffins. I still haven't heard from them, but if they pick me, it would be excellent for business.

But back to Abby. Claiming that I've mistaken her order is a trick she plays once a month, and it always gets her a free lunch. Not that Abby can't afford to pay for her sandwich. Secretly, I think she gets her kicks by thinking she's pulled the wool over my eyes.

"I'm pretty certain you ordered the tuna," I say with as much tact as I can muster.

Abby's blue eyes widen. It's the first time I've ever challenged her, and I think she's shocked.

I'm shocked too. I have a rep for always being upbeat and avoiding confrontation. Typically, on any other day of any other month, I'd apologize and offer to get her the right sandwich. But tomorrow is the grand opening of the town's new rec center. Sarah and I are providing muffins for the event. It's a big job for us, so we stayed up all night baking. I'm tired, my feet hurt, and frankly, enough is enough.

"Maybe Abby is getting dementia," says Betty Jean Collins from the next table.

Betty Jean is a regular here too. She comes in most mornings with the other members of the Gray Flamingos, a local citizens activist group for the retired bunch. Betty Jean is originally from Boston and came to north Florida a few years ago to escape the cold. She's been divorced a bunch of times and is a rabid Red Sox fan, as well as a prepper. She lives for disaster and is not-so-secretly bummed that we haven't had to evacuate for a hurricane this year.

Sitting beside her is the president of the Gray Flamingos, Viola Pantini, and her boyfriend, Gus Pappas. Viola and Gus are two of my favorite customers. Viola is a retired schoolteacher who now runs a yoga class for the active and mature adult (she hates the word seniors), and Gus owns a plumbing company. He's also a member of the city council. They're both widowed and have been dating for a couple of years. The whole town is hoping they'll get married because not only would that mean a party and free cake; everyone agrees that they're perfect for one another.

"Dementia?" sputters Abby. "My mind is as clear as day, Betty Jean Collins!"

Before Betty Jean says something back that might cause a rumble, Viola intervenes to make peace. "Abby, will you be going to the big grand opening of the rec center tomorrow?" she asks sweetly.

"Naturally. Isn't the whole town?"

A few years ago, the town's old senior center was demolished to make way for a new state of the art twenty-first-century community rec center, making Whispering Bay the envy of every small town in the Florida panhandle. Add to that the beautiful beaches, top-notch schools, and almost no existent crime rate, and Whispering Bay isn't just the Safest City in America (the town's PR slogan), we're just the best place to live. Period.

The big grand opening celebration will include free food, games, tours, and a much-anticipated costume contest. The costume theme is sixties beach movies, which is perfect for Whispering Bay since we're a beach community and the sixties is the decade that half our population considers their heyday.

"Are you going in costume?" I ask Abby.

"Naturally," she sniffs. "I'm going as Annette Funicello."

Rats. "Me too."

Going as the most famous actress from the sixties beach movies era probably isn't the most original idea, but to hear that Abby is also going as Annette is a little depressing. Although to be honest, I can't wait to see how she plans to pull that off because I've never seen her wear anything but tweed skirts and pearls. It's like she dresses as if she lives in the Scottish Highlands instead of a laid-back beach community.

"How about you, Betty Jean?" I ask. "Are you dressing up?"

Before Betty Jean can respond, the door to the café opens and her face lights up faster than a flea on steroids. Since we're not in the throes of a natural disaster, this can only mean one thing. A man has just walked into The Bistro.

Betty Jean is eighty but to call her a cougar would be underwhelming. She's more like a T-Rex, or a raptor. To her, anything male, still breathing, and under the age of sixty is fair game.

I glance over to see who's come in. It's my brother Sebastian and his best friend, Will Cunningham. Sebastian is wearing his collar, but even if he weren't, he'd still give off the priest vibe.

Will, on the other hand, is...

Honestly, I really can't be objective when it comes to Will because I've been in love with him ever since I was seven and he saved me from a pack of ravenous squirrels.

He's handsome in a quiet, smart kind of way (think

Henry Cavill playing Clark Kent), loves to read (he's a librarian), and has a great sense of humor. Plus, he always smells delicious. Like the freshly printed pages in a brand new book you want to put up to your face and inhale.

He's also the only person I've never caught in a lie.

Which isn't to say that Will doesn't lie, because I'm sure he does. But I absolutely cannot tell. Which can only mean one thing.

He must be my soul mate.

Too bad he's never gotten on board with that. To Will, I'm nothing more than Sebastian's geeky little sister with the frizzy dark hair and glasses. He wears glasses too, but on him, they look sexy.

Technically, Will is Sebastian's best friend, but when Sebastian went away to seminary, Will and I started hanging out, and over the years, he's become my best friend too.

Three months ago, Will loaned me the money for my share of the down payment to buy this place. Which was awfully nice of him, but it also means I'm in his debt and I won't feel like things are square between us until I've paid him back every single penny. He's the head librarian at the Whispering Bay Public Library, so he makes a decent living, but he's not rich.

When I asked him where he got the money, he told me a relative left it to him, but the whole thing felt fuzzy. Was it a lie? Maybe. Maybe not. Like I said, I can't tell.

They order their lunch from Sarah, who's working the counter, and I turn my attention back to Abby. "If you don't like the tuna, I'll be happy to get you something else. But I'm pretty sure you did order it. Just sayin'."

She's about to protest when I hear a squeaking sound. I look down at the large tote laying on the seat next to her and I swear, it moves.

She notices my reaction. "The tuna sandwich is fine. No problem. Just move along." To emphasize her point, she shoos me away with her hand.

Apparently, hiding whatever is in the bag is more important to her than the chance for a free sandwich.

I continue staring at the bag and, yes, there is definitely something alive in there. You didn't need any special skills here to figure out that she's lying.

"Hey, Lucy Goosey." Will plunks his tall frame down at the table adjacent from Abby's.

My brother kisses me on the cheek in greeting, and as usual, a solemn hush descends upon the café as the rest of the patrons murmur their hellos. He makes a sweeping gesture to the crowd (I think he's practicing in case he's Pope one day) then spies Abby and nods curtly. "Miss Delgado, how are you?"

"Father McGuffin," Abby replies coldly. "I'd be perfectly fine. If a certain person would only do his job."

Sebastian stiffens. "We've been through this before. I'm not the kind of priest who performs exorcisms."

Exorcisms?

A vision of Linda Blair and all that disgusting pea soup flashes through my brain. Ugh.

"Then maybe St. Perpetua's needs a real priest," she

says. "Maybe I should contact the bishop. I'm sure he'd have a thing or two to say about your behavior."

"I didn't know you were Catholic," I say to Abby.

"Well, there you go. You don't know everything, do you?"

I'm about to give in and ask Abby why on earth she needs an exorcism performed when I hear a yipping sound. Will hears it too because he points to her tote and asks, "You got a dog in there?"

Abby picks up the bag as if to move it, but a little tan head pushes its way out.

"Oh!" I automatically go to pull the dog out of the tote, but Abby snatches up the little pup and presses it against her bosom. He licks her chin and she smiles down at him, which is kind of a miracle because Abby isn't a smiley kind of person.

"He's my...service animal." The dog is maybe fifteen pounds. He looks like a Chihuahua, only bigger.

"Okay, but you know, we allow dogs here at The Bistro. There's no reason to hide him." I scratch his ears and he licks the back of my hand. He's looking at me with soulful brown eyes that smack of intelligence. I nearly melt into the floor, he's so dang cute.

I've always wanted a dog, but I'm allergic to fur, so, there you go.

I notice he's not wearing a collar. "What's his name?"

"His name?" Her eyes get a wild look in them. "His name is...Paco. Yes, that's it. Paco."

"Hey, Paco," I croon, knowing full well that's a lie, but what can I say? "You are one adorable baby."

Paco's tail wags furiously. Abby stuffs him back in her tote.

"I didn't know you had a dog," says Viola. "When did you get him?"

"Not that it's any of your business, Viola," says Abby, "but Taco belongs to my brother. I'm watching him while Derrick's away on vacation."

"I thought you said he was your service animal and that his name was Paco," says Will.

"Paco... Taco... What does it matter?" She gets up, clutching the tote protectively against her chest like she's afraid someone is going to snatch it from her. "I need to find a new place to eat lunch. One where they get your order right," she says, glaring at me. "And where the other customers aren't so dang nosy!"

We all watch as Abby stomps out of the café. The last thing I see is Paco's little face with the shiny bright eyes sticking out of the tote.

Sarah brings Will and Sebastian their food. "What's gotten into her?"

"It's the dementia," Betty Jean says with a sigh. "It'll get us all eventually."

On that happy note, Will starts eating his turkey sandwich, but Sebastian just stares down at his plate.

"What was all that about an exorcism?" I ask.

His dark eyes look troubled. "Nothing."

Betty Jean, who must have the best hearing aids in

town, because neither Sebastian nor I are speaking that loudly, says, "I bet it has something to do with her challenging Phoebe Van Cleave as head of the Sunshine Ghost Society. Abby is still convinced that there's a ghost haunting the land that the rec center was built on. Maybe she wants to drive the devil out of it."

Everyone within hearing distance moans.

A few years back there was a rumor circulating town that a spirit was haunting the old senior center. The Sunshine Ghost Society held a séance in hopes of flushing out the ghost, but of course, nothing happened, and the building was torn down to make way for the city's new rec center.

"Let's not talk about ghosts or exorcisms or Abby Delgado anymore," says Viola, "Let's talk about something happy."

Sarah breaks out in a grin. "Then that would include my new niece and nephew." Sarah is a newlywed and her sister-in-law, Whispering Bay's mayor, Mimi Grant, delivered twins a few days ago. Sarah is just a few years older than me. She's blonde and beautiful, and she and her husband Luke make the perfect couple. Sarah also makes the best macaroni and cheese I've ever tasted. She passes around her cell phone so that Viola and Betty Jean can gush over the pictures of the babies. The men all smile politely.

"How are the new parents doing?" Viola asks.

"This isn't their first rodeo," Sarah says, referring to the fact that Mimi and her husband, Zeke Grant, the town's police chief, already have a college-age daughter and a son in middle school, "but it's a bit of a shocker having two at once."

"I'll say." Gus sets down his coffee. "Good thing we voted to let Zeke hire extra help." By we, I can only assume Gus is referring to himself and the rest of the city council.

"*Wait*," says Betty Jean. "Are you telling me there's a new cop in town?"

"Yep. Officer Travis Fontaine. Good guy. Comes to us from Texas. He started this morning."

Betty Jean smirks, and since we all know the way her mind works, we cringe. "Texas, huh?"

Gus nods. "Dallas area. Lots of big city experience. We're lucky to get him. His dad retired here a few months ago. Travis is his only kin."

"James Fontaine," Sebastian adds. "New parishioner."

"Good for Zeke," Viola says. "That'll give him more time to spend with Mimi and the babies." She smiles at me. "Lucy, who will you be dressing up as tomorrow?"

"Annette Funicello."

Viola is too polite to say *you too?* Instead, she says, "I can't wait to see your costume."

"How about you?" I ask my brother. "Are you going to enter the contest?"

"I hadn't thought about it. Probably not."

The little hairs on the back of my neck start to tingle.

Sebastian has the worst tell in the world. He does this funny thing with his right eye that he's not aware of. But there it is. He's absolutely going in costume. Why he's trying to hide it from me, I have no idea.

I smirk. "You should. The prize is a hundred bucks."

He gauges my reaction and sighs because he knows he's gotten caught.

Sebastian knows all about my little "gift," but he has no idea just how talented I am. It's something I try not to talk about. Even with him.

Everyone begins talking about the big grand opening of the rec center tomorrow, and what they're wearing for the costume contest, but I can't help but be distracted by the pensive look on my brother's face.

Something isn't right.

And that something has to do with Abby Delgado.

CHAPTER TWO

I STARE at myself in the mirror and cringe.

My hair looks like:

A) A grenade has gone off inside my head and it didn't have anywhere else to go but straight up.

B) Like it belongs to a character from a Dr. Seuss book.

Or

C) Both.

I choose C.

Last week when I was putting together my outfit for the celebration, I needed some visual inspiration, so I rented the old sixties movie *Beach Blanket Bingo*, which is completely false advertising because not once do those wholesome horny teenagers ever play Bingo. I also use the word "teenager" loosely because I don't think any of the actors were a day under thirty.

To get my costume right, I asked Lauren Miller for advice. Lauren is married to Dr. Nate, one of the two practicing physicians in our town, and owns Baby Got Bump, the business next door to The Bistro. She designs retro maternity wear, but before that, she ran a retro boutique.

She loaned me a lime green shift with a matching print scarf that I've tied around my neck. Because I'm going to be on my feet all day I opted for white tennis shoes and ankle socks. My dark shoulder-length hair was supposed to be styled to flip up on the ends *ala* Annette, but something went wrong. I must have gone overboard with the teasing because my hair is ginormous. It's so big I don't think I'll be able to fit my head inside the minivan we use for the business.

I've also used so much hairspray that I should probably be wearing a flammable warning label pinned to my chest. Good thing I did all my baking yesterday so I don't have to go near a stove.

My partner Sarah is completely rocking the Sandra Dee look with a crisp white sleeveless button-down blouse, jeans, ponytail and saddle oxfords.

"You look fabulous!" Sarah squeals.

I could look like a raccoon and Sarah would still think I look good because she's the kind of person who always looks for the positive in any situation. "Thanks. So do you. Do you think my hair looks okay?"

"Sure! Er, do you want me to try to flatten it some?"

Obviously, she too is afraid that I won't fit into the minivan.

Sarah does her best to bring my hair down a few inches,

but it's like trying to move a hundred-pound rock. "How much hairspray did you use?"

"I don't know. Half a can maybe?"

She giggles. "Lucy, have you ever used hairspray before in your life?"

"Yes."

She looks dubious.

"Okay," I admit. "Just once. High school. Senior year prom."

She shrugs, then smiles. "No worries. You look fabulous. No one's hair is going to look this terrific. You might just win the costume contest!"

I've caught Sarah in a few fibs before, but this isn't one of them. She honestly believes this, so I smile back at her.

We load up the back of the minivan with over twenty-four dozen carefully packed muffins. There are six varieties —double chocolate chip, banana nut, blueberry (*yawn*), lemon poppy seed, oat bran (remember, we have a large retired population here in town) and my hands-down most popular ever—the apple walnut cream cheese muffin.

I worked on perfecting the recipe for almost a year. It's my signature muffin. Plus, it's Will's favorite, so it holds a special place in my heart. It's also the recipe I used for my *Muffin Wars* audition tape, which, I'm kind of worried about now because if they pick me, I'll have to bake something different, and not to brag or anything but I would totally win with the apple walnut cream cheese.

We finish packing everything up then head to the rec center. The sun peeks over the horizon, throwing an orange haze over the crystal-clear blue water of the Gulf of Mexico. It's early November and sixty degrees, with a projected high of only seventy-four. A beautiful north Florida fall day, perfect to celebrate the town's new state of the art recreational center. There's an indoor and outdoor basketball court, two swimming pools, tennis courts, classrooms and my favorite feature, a humongous gourmet kitchen. Sarah and I have already been approached about teaching cooking classes. I'm also thinking of heading up a community garden.

Even though it's barely seven a.m. and the festivities don't start for another two hours, the place is swarming. The Gray Flamingos are acting as event "hosts" and will be doing tours. Most of them are in costume, but a few of them are wearing their Gray Power T-shirts. There will be arts and crafts for the kiddies, free food and lots of fun.

Heidi from Heidi's Bakery is setting up her booth right next to ours. Her donuts are legendary. If you're into donuts, that is.

"Yoo-hoo!" Heidi waves and Sarah and I wave back. "Gorgeous day, isn't it?"

"Sure is!" says Sarah.

Viola and Betty Jean come by to check out our booth. Betty Jean is wearing a black wig (which looks better than her regular hair), capris and ballet flats. "Look, Lucy! We're both Annettes!"

I try my best to smile. *Great*. Another Annette Funicello.

Viola is wearing a dress with a cinch belt that flares at

the hips. Her chin-length salt and pepper hair is teased and sprayed. She's also wearing a pair of awesome cat style glasses with little rhinestones at the corners. "I'm going as a sixties school teacher. Believe it or not, I used to wear this back in the day."

Gus, who is dressed as a surfer dude (board shorts, Hawaiian shirt, and flip-flops), guides us to the back door of the building. He pulls a set of keys from his pocket. "We're keeping the building locked till the tours start. Don't want anyone jumping the gun and getting a peek inside till after the big ribbon-cutting ceremony." He unlocks the door for us. "Never thought this day would come, but here we are."

"What do you mean?" Sarah asks.

"Between us, this building isn't one hundred percent operational yet, but the city council didn't want to delay the opening celebration since we'd advertised it so heavily."

I glance around. "Everything looks good to me."

"It's nothing major. Just some details that need to be ironed out. Security cameras, temperature controls on the swimming pool, basketball equipment that hasn't come in yet, that kind of stuff."

The door leads straight into the kitchen. Gus turns on the lights and helps us place two large industrial coffee makers onto a cart to take out to our food station. Besides doling out muffins, we'll be making coffee.

I catch Gus staring at my hair.

"I know. It's a kind of big."

"No, it looks great," he says.

Ouch. That was such a lie.

We wheel the cart back to our food booth. Sarah and I finish setting up the muffins and start the coffee brewing. The volunteer crowd is getting bigger. Jenna Pantini, the city manager, comes by and checks out our display. "Oh my God, you brought the apple walnut cream cheese muffins!" She looks at them longingly, so I offer her one. "I really shouldn't." But she takes it anyway.

Jenna goes off to check on the rest of the food vendors. Soon it's nine a.m., and the celebration is underway. In no time the entire outdoor area is packed with people. I've seen at least a dozen Annettes and Frankies already. It looks like everyone in town got their cue from *Beach Blanket Bingo*.

Sarah and I are giving out muffins and chit chatting with the locals when an entourage from the Sunshine Ghost Society comes sniffing up to our booth. They are minus Abby, which is a relief. After yesterday's scene in The Bistro, I'm not anxious to run into her again. At least, not until Sebastian explains what's going on between them.

Phoebe Van Cleave is the head of their group and a real nutcase, but her brother Roger owns the local paper, and he's a total sweetheart, so I try to be nice to her for his sake. She's dressed as a hippie, which I must admit is a fun take on the whole sixties thing, even if it doesn't exactly say beach movie.

I check out the rest of the costumes, then do a double take when my gaze lands on Gloria Hightower. She's the group medium, and according to Phoebe, she's the best. Gloria's naturally blonde hair has lots of gray, but today she's wearing a black wig because of course, she, too, is dressed as Annette Funicello.

"What a coincidence!" she says. "We're both Annette!"

I smile wearily. "Yeah, neat, huh? How do you like the festival so far?"

"Oh, everything is just wonderful." Gloria looks over at the main rec center building with shiny eyes. "I can't wait till the tours begin. You know the site is haunted, don't you?"

"If there's a ghost haunting the new building, then Gloria will feel it right away," Phoebe says.

Gloria blushes. "Well, not *right* away. But, I am pretty good, even if I say so myself."

"Have you heard from the people at *Muffin Wars*?" asks Victor Marino. He's in his late sixties and recently retired from a forty-year career at the post office, and yes, he's dressed as Frankie. He's an Atlanta Braves fan (me too!), and he always leaves a nice chunk of change in my tip jar.

"Not yet," I admit.

"You'll get picked. And when you go on T.V., you need to make your mango coconut muffin. The judges will love it."

I wish I felt as confident as Victor. The mango coconut muffin project is something I've been working on for the past couple of months. Victor was in The Bistro the day I gave out samples of version number three. Everyone raved about it, but it's still not quite right, and I can't put it on the menu until it's perfect.

"We're all keeping our fingers crossed for you," says

Phoebe eyeing my muffin display. "They all look delicious! Which one should I try?"

"For you? The oat bran."

The oat bran has been our least popular today, and we need to get rid of them. Plus, I'm sure Phoebe's diet could use the extra roughage.

Phoebe bites into her muffin and makes the yummy face. I offer the rest of her group muffins and they all jump on the boring blueberry.

The morning goes by quickly. We're down to just two muffins when an amused male voice asks, "What's going on with your hair?"

It's Will. And *holy wow* he looks good.

He's wearing a striped bathing suit and a white button-down shirt. His dark hair is slicked back, and he's not wearing his glasses so when he smiles you can see the skin around his blue eyes crinkle, which is completely adorable. He told me a few days ago he'd be dressing as the James Darren character from the *Gidget* movies and he's nailed it. Will puts the moon in Moondoggie like no one else.

I try to act very cool. "So, you like my hair, huh?"

He gives it a hard look. "You're going to need help taking that thing down. You might even need a hammer."

Sarah sniffs. "I think Lucy looks great."

"So do I." This comes from someone I don't recognize. Except...

Oh no.

I try not to laugh. My brother is decked out from head

to toe in leather and has a silly cap on his head. No wonder he didn't want to talk about his costume.

"Please don't tell me you're Eric Von Zipper."

"I saw the movie too," Sebastian says dryly.

In *Beach Blanket Bingo* Eric Von Zipper is the head of the motorcycle gang that doesn't like the surfers. The fact that my brother, the priest, is going as a sixties beach movie villain is pretty funny.

Sebastian *aka* Eric takes the last of the apple walnut cream cheese muffins, but I don't begrudge him that because he's my brother and I love him. Plus, he didn't make fun of my hair.

While we're chatting, an older distinguished looking gentleman joins our group. "Hello, Father," he says, nodding at Sebastian. Sebastian introduces him as James Fontaine, the new parishioner he'd mentioned yesterday at lunch. He just bought a house on Seville Street near Viola.

"Call me Jim." He shakes my hand with a firm grip. "Interesting festival. Very, uh, colorful costumes, too." He's a big guy, maybe six foot three with a full head of white hair and sparkly green eyes.

I love green eyes. Green is the color of everything good —grass, lime flavored jelly beans, money... You get my drift. If he's poking fun at my costume, I don't mind, because, yes, I have to admit, my hair does look ridiculous.

"Lucy makes the best muffins in the world," Sebastian boasts. "She's going to be on T.V. and everything."

I flush. I almost wish I'd kept the *Muffin Wars* thing to myself. What if I don't make the cut? Then everyone in town will feel sorry for me, and I'd hate that. "The T.V. thing isn't a done deal yet." I hand Jim my card. "Sarah and I own a little café here in town. The Bistro by the Beach. First muffin is on the house."

He pockets the card and smiles at me, and something in my chest goes fuzzy warm because I know in that instant that Jim is going to become not just one of my favorite customers, but one of my favorite people. This is another gift I have. Call it my Spidey sense. I'm great at reading people and my first impression is *always* spot on.

"Jim used to be a homicide detective with the Dallas Police," says Sebastian.

Will perks up. "Really?"

"It's a lot more boring than it sounds," Jim says.

"Jim is being modest. He's worked on some really big cases and has even been on T.V. Maybe he can give you some pointers when you get picked to be on *Muffin Wars*, Lucy."

"What show were you on, Jim?" I ask.

He shrugs like he's embarrassed by all the attention we're giving him. "*America's Most Vicious Criminals*."

"*Holy wow*! Will and I watch that show all the time. What episode? I bet we've seen it."

Will is looking at Jim the way I look at chocolate chip muffins. *America's Most Vicious Criminals* is his favorite show. Every Friday night Will comes over to my place with a pizza from Tiny's (best pizza in Whispering Bay), and we watch it together, but last night's episode was a rerun, so we skipped our usual routine.

Jim clears his throat. "I was the lead investigator in a case involving a nurse in the Dallas Fort Worth area who—"

"The media referred to her as the Angel of Death," Will supplies eagerly. "She killed six patients. About...fifteen years ago. Right?"

How Will remembers every episode in such minute detail, I have no idea.

"That's right." A shadow crosses Jim's face. I don't have Will's memory for this stuff, but I'm pretty sure it's one of those cases where they failed to apprehend the murderer.

Before Jim can say anything else, Sebastian changes the subject. "I hear that your son has just joined our local police force."

"Travis is a good kid. Well, he's thirty, so hardly a kid. Just moved out here this week. I guess he thought his old man needed some company in his retirement."

Jim's casual words can't hide the great love I feel this man has for his son. Personally, I think it's really sweet of this Travis guy to move to be close to his father. Since Whispering Bay is such a small town and all the cops get their coffee at my café, I'll meet him eventually. If he's anything like Jim, I'm sure Travis and I will be great friends.

"What made you retire in Whispering Bay?" I ask.

"I came here on my honeymoon thirty-five years ago. My wife loved it. We always talked about moving here, but she passed last year."

I cringe. "I'm so sorry."

He smiles kindly. "Thank you."

Everyone murmurs words of condolences, but now that

I've put my size eight sneaker into my mouth, the mood has soured. Sebastian and Jim excuse themselves to explore the rest of the food booths, leaving Sarah and me alone with Will.

"Oh, Lucy, look! We're out of coffee," says Sarah, like this is a national emergency. "You should go to the kitchen for more supplies. I'd help you, but I *hate* to leave the booth without one of us here."

Sarah is only one of the two people that I've told about my Will crush. My face goes hot at her blatant attempt to throw us together.

Luckily, Will seems oblivious to Sarah's machinations. "Want some help?" he asks.

Even though I don't need help, I'm about to say yes, when who pops into my booth? None other than my arch-nemesis, Brittany Kelly.

CHAPTER THREE

"HEY, LUCY!" she chirps like she's ecstatic to see me, and even this is a lie because Brittany Kelly can't stand my guts. She's still mad that I called her out in kindergarten for stealing the paint brushes. From Girl Scouts to high school, she's made my life miserable. In a completely passive aggressive way, because to the rest of the world, Brittany is the epitome of the beautiful sweet southern deb.

"Hey, Brittany!" I mimic back.

She's wearing a skin-tight sequined gown, and her auburn hair is artfully arranged in a flattering up do. Even though we're outside on the grass, she's wearing four-inch heels. It's like she's reviving her look from prom night when she was crowned queen.

"What an interesting costume," Sarah muses.

"You like it?" Brittany slowly circles around so we can admire her assets (literally).

"Who are you supposed to be?" Will asks. Although

Will has never said it aloud, I know he finds Brittany attractive. His whole body practically *hums* whenever she's around.

"The movie star from *Gilligan's Island*. Technically I suppose it's not a *movie* character, but I don't think you can get more sixties beachy than Ginger."

"You look cute," Sarah concedes, because she's honest, and yes, Brittany is killing the Ginger look.

"Thanks, Sarah!" Her eyes get a sparkly look in them. Brittany has brown eyes, but they're not regular brown eyes like mine. They're so light that sometimes you think they're green and other times you aren't sure. They're her best feature. And she knows it. Besides her hair. She also has incredible hair. And an adorable nose and a gorgeous figure and...

The whole thing is so unfair.

"Lucy," Brittany says. "Who are you dressed as?"

I would think it was apparent, but I fake smile and say, "Annette Funicello."

"Oh." She pauses for effect. "You should have told me you were having trouble coming up with something original. We could have coordinated outfits. You would have been an *adorable* Mary Ann!"

Right. Not that Mary Ann wasn't attractive, but the way Brittany emphasizes the word adorable it's like Mary Ann was Ginger's pet hamster. She would have probably insisted I wear baggy overalls and had straw sticking out of my hair.

"By the way, Lucy, I saw your audition tape for *Muffin Wars*. I've got my fingers crossed for you!"

"*What?* I mean...how is that possible?" I sputter.

"Daddy has a friend who works for The Cooking Channel, and when he came across an audition tape from someone local, he called Daddy to find out all about you. Naturally, Daddy put in a good word for you."

Great. Now if I get on the show, I'll have to wonder if it's because they really liked my muffins or if it's because of Brittany's dad pulling strings on my behalf.

Brittany's family owns The Harbor House, Whispering Bay's fanciest restaurant. I worked there washing dishes during the summers while I was in high school. At first, I thought it was cool of Brittany's dad to give me a job, but in hindsight, I think it was just so that Brittany could lord it over me at school. Still, it was a good experience. Even though the work was hard, it's where I discovered my passion for baking.

You'd think growing up in the restaurant business, Brittany would feel the same way too. But not only does she have no interest, her culinary skills amount to zilch. "I can't even boil an egg!" I heard her brag one day as if this is something to be proud of.

Brittany went to Florida State University where she majored in sorority princess and marketing. After graduation, her daddy got her a job on the Chamber of Commerce doing PR for the city. She's the one who came up with the Safest City in America tagline that everyone thinks is so wonderful. I hate to admit it, but it's not half bad.

Brittany says in a staged low voice that everyone can still hear, "Lucy, can I give you some pointers? If you get picked to be on T.V., and I mean, *of course,* you'll get picked, you might want to lose a little weight. The camera always adds ten pounds."

"I think Lucy looks really healthy," Will says in my defense.

I study Will carefully for any signs of deception, but there's...nothing. These are the times I wish I knew if Will was telling the truth or just lying to be nice. Because if he's telling the truth, maybe it means he finds me attractive. Which means maybe I have a chance with him. On the other hand, "healthy" could also be interpreted to mean something entirely different.

"Oh, Will," Brittany says in a little girl voice that grates on my nerves, "Lucy is so lucky to have you for a friend!" She bats her lashes at him then proceeds to bore us with details of her last vacation. To be fair, the trip was to Paris. But instead of telling us about all the wonderful French food she ate and the interesting places she got to visit, all she talks about is the great shopping.

Ugh. I don't think I can stand much more of this.

"I can get the coffee by myself," I mutter even though no one's paying attention to me.

I search the grounds until I find Gus, who's over by the main stage. He and some of the other Gray Flamingos are in the middle of counting votes for the costume contest. I'm still holding onto hope that I win. I mean, yes, there are a lot of Annettes here, but half of them are wearing wigs. No one's hair is as big as mine. Surely that must count for *something*.

"I hate to bother you, but can you open the kitchen door for me again? I have to replenish the coffee cart."

"Here, you can have the keys." Gus reaches into his pocket and comes up empty. He gazes around the table and frowns. "I know I put them somewhere."

Viola patiently searches until she finds them. "Sorry! Things have been so disorganized. The one for the kitchen door has a red dot on it."

"Thanks!"

I wheel the empty food cart into the building and make my way to the kitchen. I'm almost finished gathering the supplies we'll need to replenish the coffee station when I hear a familiar whimpering sound. I turn and see a little tan dog huddled in the corner.

"Paco! What are you doing here?" I scoop him up and clutch him to my chest. He's trembling. How on earth did Abby's dog get inside the building? She wasn't with the other members of the Sunshine Ghost Society who came by the booth, but she must be here at the festivities.

Maybe she's avoiding me after yesterday's brouhaha over the tuna salad sandwich.

Whatever. She'll just have to get over it.

"Are you okay, little guy?" Paco licks my hand, but he's still trembling. "Let's go find your momma."

I leave the cart inside the kitchen and walk out into the sunshine. There are even more people here now than before. Combing through the crowd, I see lots of familiar faces, but no sign of Abby.

Sarah is probably wondering what's keeping me. I

should probably take Paco back to the food booth. Maybe Sarah can watch him until Abby shows up. My eyes are itching, and my nose is running. There's absolutely no doubt that I'm allergic to this sweet little dog.

I weave our way through the crowd. I'm almost back to the food pavilion when Paco starts struggling against me. Before I can stop him, he leaps from my arms and runs away.

Blast! What if he takes off for the beach? Or worse, the road? If anything happens to Paco, I'll never forgive myself, so I run after him. Good thing I'm wearing tennis shoes.

He's almost back to the building when I trip over a hibiscus bush and land face first in the dirt. Luckily, the bush cushioned my weight so that I'm not hurt, but there's blood dripping from my elbow. I straighten up and brush the dirt off my face and feel my hair for any damage. Even though I can't see myself, I'm confident there's not a hair out of place. Maybe all that hairspray wasn't such a bad idea after all.

Paco is waiting for me by a side door to the building. He's panting (yeah, me too, buddy) like he's out of breath and looking at me with those adorable eyes of his like he's trying to tell me something.

"You want to go back inside?" A part of me feels foolish talking to him like he can understand me, but he wags his tail and barks as if he's answering.

"I'll take that as a yes. But this is the wrong door, sweetie."

There must be at least eight keys on this ring. I have no

idea which one will open this particular door. On a whim, I place my hand over the knob and Paco yelps in excitement, like he's encouraging me on.

I turn the knob, and the door opens.

Huh. That's weird. I thought Gus said all the doors were supposed to be locked.

I walk into a small room filled with boxes, which leads me to think this is a storage area. Since I'm here, I might as well head back to the kitchen to collect the coffee cart.

Except Paco takes off running. *Again.* Which is really annoying.

At least this time there are no bushes to trip over.

"Paco!" I yell. "Come back this instant!"

I search the kitchen but he's not there, so I make my way into the large main room. There's a table set up with balloons and flyers in anticipation of the tours, but there's no sign of Paco.

Then I hear the sound of his toe nails clicking against the tile floors. "I hear you!" My voice echoes in the vast empty building.

Paco barks in response like we're playing a game.

I follow the sound through a hallway and into an empty classroom.

"Ha! I found you!"

Paco sits there patiently like he's been waiting for me to show up. Then he looks down at something, and it takes me a few seconds to realize what it is.

It's Abby.

She's lying perfectly still like she's asleep, only...there's a little puddle of blood on the floor next to her head.

Oh my God.

I crouch next to her and shake her arm. "Abby, are you all right?"

Paco looks at me with those big eyes like he's begging me to help her. It's been a while since I took a CPR course and I've never had to use it, but I don't think the basics have changed.

I check to make sure Abby is breathing, which, she's not. Then I check the vein in her neck for a pulse and my own pulse goes wildly out of control.

I push up the sleeve of her sweater and check her wrist to make sure I haven't made a mistake.

But I haven't.

It looks as if I don't have to worry about Abby holding the tuna salad sandwich incident over my head because Abby isn't asleep.

She's dead.

CHAPTER FOUR

"LUCY, ARE YOU SURE?" Will asks.

"There's no pulse, and she's not breathing. So yeah, I'm pretty sure she's dead." I shudder. Poor Abby. What was she doing inside the rec center? Since I didn't have my cell phone on me, the only thing I could do was run back to the food pavilion to get help.

Will notifies the cops, then he, Sarah and Brittany all follow me back inside the building.

Why Brittany has to tag along, I have no idea. It's not like she's going to be a big help or anything. She takes one step into the room and stops cold. "Oh my God," she whimpers. "This is my classroom."

"What do you mean, your classroom?" I ask.

"Didn't I tell you? I just got my Pilates teaching certificate. I'm going to be leading the 8 p.m. class on Tuesday and Thursdays." She closes one eye as she peers at Abby.

"I've never seen a dead person before. I mean, other than at a wake."

Neither have I.

Other than the puddle of blood by her head, Abby looks like she does on every other normal day that she walks into The Bistro for lunch. The whole thing is eerie. We stand there staring down at her like a bunch of rubberneckers.

I'm still holding Paco. His shivering has subsided, but he has to be traumatized. "Poor little guy," I mutter, holding him tightly. "He must have been with Abby when she fell."

"Is that what you think happened?" asks Sarah.

"I guess so. She must have been looking around then slipped and hit her head."

Nobody else says anything until the cops show up. It's Rusty Newton and, Thank God, Zeke Grant is with him. Rusty has been on the Whispering Bay police force since forever. He's a good old boy and super sweet, but think Barney Fife from the old Andy Griffith show, and you'll know why I'm happy that Zeke is here too.

"What happened?" Zeke asks in a quiet, authoritative voice.

I explain how I found Abby.

"Rusty," Zeke says, "Tell Jenna to cancel the tours. And call Travis. I left him at the security tent, but I think we're going to need him here."

"Aye-aye, chief!" As morbid as this sounds, Rusty looks more excited than when I put the lemon poppy seed muffins on sale last week. Those are his favorite, and he stops by The Bistro every morning to get one along with his cup of coffee.

"I thought you'd be home with Mimi and the babies," I say to Zeke while Rusty makes the call.

"I dropped by to make sure the security detail was running smoothly," Zeke explains. "I have a new cop on the force with lots of experience, so I'm going to let him handle this." He asks us all not to touch anything. Then he says his goodbyes.

Rusty walks around Abby making tsking sounds. After a few minutes, a new cop appears on the scene. This must be the infamous Travis Fontaine we've heard so much about.

He's tall, with dark blond hair and green eyes like his father. He meets my gaze, but there's none of his father's friendliness or warmth. Instead, his eyes cut through me like razor blades. He looks at Abby then back at me. Any second now I expect fire to come snorting out his nose.

"Are you the one who found Miss Delgado?" he asks in a deep voice with a healthy dose of Texas. A little shiver of *something* runs up my spine. Attraction? *No*. That can't be it. Must be leftover tension from finding poor Abby dead.

"Lucy McGuffin. That's me."

"I'm Officer Travis Fontaine." He stares at my hair for a second, blinks, then eyes the rest of the group. "Can I have your names, please?"

Before anyone else can introduce themselves, Brittany begins to whimper. "I thought...that is..." She gasps like she can't catch her breath. "I think I'm going to faint..." And then in a dramatic swoon, she begins her descent to the ground in slow motion.

Both Travis and Will lunge for her, but Travis is faster.

Even though she's fainting (or whatever it is she's doing), Brittany manages to collapse gracefully into Travis's arms. I have to give her credit. She's good.

"Miss, are you all right?" Travis looks down at her with concern.

"I'm... Oh, yes! Thank you so much, *Officer!*" Only Brittany could make a mundane word like "officer" sound sexy.

Travis carefully sets her on her feet like she's a delicate piece of china he's afraid will break.

Sarah secures Brittany by the elbow as Will rustles up a folding chair. Her movie star gown is so tight I wonder how she'll manage to sit without splitting a seam. She folds herself into the chair, and nothing pops or bursts. Go, Brittany!

"Can we get her some juice?" Travis asks Rusty.

Rusty makes a disappointed face like this is beneath him, but he does what Travis asks. Frankly, I don't blame Rusty. For one thing, I'm sure he doesn't want to be bossed around by this younger cop, plus, I doubt Brittany needs the juice.

Travis gets all our names and writes everything down in a notebook. A couple of other people show up and introduce themselves. They're from the county coroner's office. One of them takes pictures. The other one scours the area for what, I don't know, but he's taking measurements. Occasionally he'll pick something up off the floor and place it inside a baggie. It occurs to me that they're making a big production over an accident. It's like we've walked straight into an episode of *CSI*.

"What made you come inside the building?" Travis asks me. "The tours aren't supposed to begin for almost another hour."

"I was in here earlier, well, in the kitchen, that is, to get supplies to make the coffee."

"And that's what you were doing? Getting more supplies?"

"At first, yes. That's how I found Paco."

"Paco?"

"The dog." I lift Paco's paw and move it up and down like he's waving. "Say hello to Officer Fontaine."

The officer in question doesn't crack a smile. Which under the circumstances is probably appropriate, but *jeez*. Whenever I'm scared or overwhelmed, I find solace in humor, but I can't imagine this guy ever smiling.

"Paco was in here by himself. At least, I thought he was by himself. He belongs to Derrick, that's Abby's brother. She's dog sitting for him. Or, she was." It just occurred to me that I can't use present tense when talking about Abby anymore. I stifle another shudder.

"And that's when you found Ms. Delgado?"

"Not at first. Paco was pretty skittish, so I picked him up to take him outside, but then he ran away from me. That's when he led me back inside the building."

"He led you back?"

I nod.

"How did he do that exactly?"

"He ran this way, and he was barking. You know, like he was talking to me. In dog speak."

There's a pause. "Are you some kind of dog expert?"

I don't like his tone of voice, but since he's a cop and I was raised to respect authority, I'll let it go. *This time.* "Actually, I'm allergic to them."

"But you're familiar with *this* particular dog?"

"Sure. Abby brought Paco to The Bistro yesterday. That's the café Sarah and I own. Only his real name isn't Paco."

He frowns. "What do you mean that's not his real name?"

Rats. Me and my big mouth. I'm not about to explain my special "gift" to Officer Fontaine. First off, I doubt he'd believe me. I've only known him ten minutes, but I can already tell this guy has a stick up his butt.

"Nothing. I must be confused. This is my first dead person, you know?"

Instead of looking concerned that I might be about to faint, he gives me a look that says he doesn't have time for any more of my monkey business. *Just the facts, ma'am.*

"Do you know Derrick's last name?" he asks.

"I've never met him. He lives in Mexico Beach, I think, but I imagine it's Delgado. Abby wasn't married."

Sarah chimes in. "Lucy is right. It's Derrick Delgado. I haven't met him either, but I've heard her mention him a few times."

"Do any of you know how we might reach him?"

We all shake our heads.

He begins to question the rest of the group. The photographer finishes taking pictures. Then a couple of guys come in with a gurney.

"Will that be all, Officer Fontaine?" Sarah asks. "I need to get back to the food pavilion."

"Can I get all of you to write down your contact numbers, please? And your addresses, in case we need them."

Here is where I want to snicker because Travis has no idea that pretty much everyone in Whispering Bay knows everyone else, as well as where to find them. But we all comply and write down our number next to our name.

"I wrote down my cell phone, my home, *and* all my business numbers," Brittany emphasizes. "Just in case you need me. For *anything*."

I cringe. Brittany's blatant flirtation is an embarrassment to womankind.

I glance at Will to gauge his reaction. He looks miserable.

If the object of Will's affection were anyone other than Brittany, I would feel sorry for him. But she's so not worthy of him. Can't he see that?

We're all about to leave, when Travis says, "Miss McGuffin, can you stay a moment? I'd like to speak to you in private."

Brittany makes a pouty face, but she follows Sarah and Will as they go out the door.

Travis stares at my hair again.

"I'm supposed to Annette Funicello," I explain. "In case you're wondering."

His eyes cut back to mine. "You said you were following the dog back into the building when you discovered the body?"

The way he says *body* puts me on alert. Like something sinister has happened here.

"Yes. But... this was an accident, right?"

"When was the last time you saw Miss Delgado?" he asks, ignoring my question.

"I already told you. She came in yesterday to The Bistro with the little dog."

"Did she seem agitated in any way?"

Yes.

"No," I lie. Because:

A) I really don't want to get into the whole sandwich thing.

B) I still don't know why Abby and Sebastian were out of sorts. Besides, none of that has anything to do with what's happened here.

Thus:

C) It's not relevant.

"You didn't see Miss Delgado at all today?"

He's already asked me this question three different ways. "No," I say again, this time in a firmer tone.

"Did you get in a fight with someone?"

"*What*? Why on earth would you think that?"

He points to the edge of my shift, which I notice has a tear. My left knee is skinned. "I already told you I chased

Paco back into the building. I tripped over a bush, and this happened."

He looks at me for a few long seconds. "Okay. Thanks for your cooperation."

The little hairs on the back of my neck tingle.

Oh boy. Officer Fontaine is lying. Well, not lying exactly but he doesn't think I'm cooperating at all. He thinks I'm hiding something. Which I am since I didn't tell him about Abby being mad at Sebastian.

"By the way," he says. "What door did you use to get inside the building?"

"The kitchen—*oh*." I pull the keys out of my pocket. "Earlier, Sarah and I came in through the kitchen with Gus Pappas, and I used the keys again to get in the second time to refill the coffee cart. But when Paco led me back, and, *yes*," I glare at him, "He did lead me back, we used a side door to get inside."

"And you used one of those keys to unlock that door too?"

"No. It was already open."

He stills. "There was a side door to the building that was open?"

"Not open exactly. Just unlocked."

"Can you show me?"

With Paco still in my arms, I lead him to the door. "Are you sure it was unlocked?" he asks. "Maybe you used one of the keys and forgot?"

I squelch the urge to roll my eyes at him. "It was unlocked," I say firmly.

He unclips his walkie-talkie and asks the technicians to return.

It's clear that Travis doesn't think Abby's death is a simple case of her falling and hitting her head. "Do you think this is how Abby got inside the building?"

"Possibly." He studies the lock. After a few minutes, he remembers that I'm still there. "Thanks, again. You can get back to whatever it was you were doing now."

In other words, *dismissed*.

Except he's not going to get rid of me this easily. Stubborn is my middle name (actually, it's Elizabeth).

"What are you looking for?"

"I really can't discuss that with you."

"Holy wow. You think that maybe someone shoved Abby and then she fell and hit her head? But that would be like...murder."

Before he can respond, the two guys who were taking pictures and collecting evidence in the building arrive.

"Are you going to sweep the place for fingerprints?" I ask one of them. His tag says *G. Cooper, Crime Scene Investigation*. "Because if you do, mine will definitely be there. Maybe you should go ahead and fingerprint me. That way you can compare the prints on the door to mine and rule those out."

G. Cooper looks confused like he's not sure whether to take my advice.

"Miss McGuffin," says Officer Fontaine, "I have to insist that you leave now."

"But—"

"Please, leave this to the professionals."

Boy, this guy sure could use a course in community relations. He's absolutely nothing like his father. And to think, I thought he and I were going to be friends. *Ha!*

I make my way back to the food pavilion. A sad hush has descended over the festivities. News of Abby's death has spread, and no one feels like celebrating anything, but the adults continue for the sake of the kiddies.

Paco has stopped his shaking. I let him down on a patch of grass so he can do his business. When I get back to our booth, Sarah has already cleaned everything up, and she and her husband Luke are loading up the back of the van.

Brittany is still hanging around, probably because of Will. "They're about to announce the winner of the costume contest!" she says.

Funny. Less than an hour ago she'd been so distraught she'd "fainted." Brittany's ability to bounce back from tragedy is impressive.

"May I have your attention!" Gus's voice booms over the loudspeaker system. "First, I want to thank everyone who came out in costume today. Good job, Whispering Bay! It was a tough competition, but there was one person who stood out for their originality. The votes are in, and the winner of the best sixties beach costume is Brittany Kelly!"

Brittany looks around in shock. "*Me?* Did he say me? Oh my God!" She runs toward the stage in her four-inch heels where Gus is waiting for her with a smile and a trophy. Not to mention her hundred-dollar check, which should keep Brittany in lip gloss for about a month.

"Thank you!" she gushes into the mic. "I'm so humbled and proud that y'all have chosen me as the winner!" Images of high school and Brittany's victory prom night speech come flashing back. I swear, I think she used those exact same words then too. It's probably her standard speech. Besides prom queen, Brittany was also Miss Seashell, Miss Walton County and last but not least, Miss Cheese Grits (although since her daddy's restaurant held the contest, I'm sure that was rigged).

"Y'all are too kind, but I simply can't accept this check." Her southern accent rises a couple of notches the way it always does whenever she's doing any public speaking. "Not when there are so many people who need it more than I do. So, if it's all right with y'all, I'd like to donate it to the food pantry at St. Perpetua's which does such a wonderful job of feeding the hungry."

Everyone claps wildly, and Roger Van Cleave takes her picture for the paper.

I'm not disappointed. I'm really not. Because if I'd won, I'd have to go up on stage in front of everyone and right now, I probably look a mess. Plus, whatever her motives, it was nice of Brittany to donate the money.

Will stares at Brittany with a dreamy look on his face.

"Earth to Cunningham," I say.

He shakes his dark head. "Sorry. I was just—"

"Admit it. You like her."

"I know she made your life miserable, Luce, but that was in high school. She's not a bad person. The thing is... I want to ask her out, but not if it's going to come between us."

I still. "Why would it come between us?" Then I laugh, and it sounds fake, but what can I do? "Ask her out! If you like her, then I like her."

The relief on his face makes me want to cry. Will has no skills when it comes to detecting deception. Either that, or he just doesn't want to see it, because this is probably the biggest lie I've ever told.

Paco nudges me with his nose like he wants attention. I'd forgotten I was still holding him.

"What are you going to do with the dog?" Will asks.

"I hate to hand him over to the animal shelter. I know they'll take good care of him until Abby's brother gets back, but he's been through a hard day."

"I'll take him," Will offers. "Since you're allergic."

This is really nice of Will, but I feel a strange kinship with this little dog, and despite my allergy, I'm just not ready to give him up yet.

"One night with him isn't going to kill me." I glance around the crowd. "Have you seen Sebastian?"

"I texted him after we found Abby, but he hasn't texted back. He probably got called away to the rectory." Will studies my face. "Are you sure you're going to be okay?"

"I'm fine."

He nods. "See you later, Lucy." Out of the corner of my eye, I watch him congratulate Brittany.

Even though the temperature is only in the mid-seventies, I'm sweating and itching. All I want right now is to go home, take a hot shower and crawl into bed.

Sarah comes back to the booth. "I don't know about you, but I'm ready to call it a day. Luke is already on his way home."

I hold Paco on my lap as Sarah drives us back to the café. Luckily, I live in the apartment upstairs which is extra convenient because I'm exhausted. I unlock the back door and start to make my way up the stairs with Paco, when Sarah says, "What some help with your hair? I mean, taking it down?"

"No thanks. I figure I'll just get in the shower and let it fall apart naturally."

She pauses. "I didn't want to say anything before, because there wasn't a point, but...don't freak out."

"What?" I ask, alarmed because naturally when someone tells you not to freak out, your first instinct is to freak out.

She bites her bottom lip, like she's not sure what to do, then sighs. "Okay, here goes." She closes her eyes as she reaches out and tears something out of my hair.

"*Ouch!*"

She winces. "Sorry about that."

"What did you do that for?"

"You had something stuck in your hair, and I wanted to get it out for you." Then she gingerly holds up a dead lizard by the tail.

"*That* was in my hair?"

She makes a pained face and nods.

"How in the world—"

The lizard must have gotten stuck in the cave of hair-spray when I tripped and fell over the hibiscus bush.

No wonder Officer Fontaine kept staring at my hair!

All the while he was asking me questions, there was a dead reptile staring right back at him.

CHAPTER FIVE

WHEN SARAH and I bought The Bistro we made a pact that the business wouldn't take over our lives, so we hired extra help and decided to close the café one day a week. Sunday seemed like the most logical day.

When you're used to getting up at four-thirty every morning, six a.m. is technically sleeping in, but today it takes a huge effort to drag out of bed in time to make my regular seven-thirty Sunday mass. It must be the aftereffects of the Benadryl I had to take last night to keep from itching.

The instant mass is over, I dash out to the front of the church hoping to have a word with my brother, but Sebastian is inundated with parishioners wanting to talk to him, so I don't get a chance to ask him about Abby and the exorcism.

"Hello, Lucy!" Jim Fontaine waves, so I wave back, which he takes as a sign to come up to talk to me. Normally, I'd welcome his company, but unfortunately, he's not alone.

"Officer" Travis is with him. He's out of uniform and wearing neatly pressed khaki pants and a blue button-down shirt that contrasts with his green eyes, making them look even greener.

I have to admit, Travis isn't bad looking. He's not classically handsome like Will, but he does exude a certain *something*. Too bad he has no personality. On the other hand, that makes him perfect for Brittany.

It was obvious yesterday that she had the hots for him. I wonder if Will had a chance to ask her out. And if she said yes. Maybe if I'm lucky, he changed his mind. And maybe if I'm really lucky, Brittany will channel all her efforts into Officer Fontaine.

Jim turns to his son. "Travis, this is Lucy McGuffin. She's Father Sebastian's sister and I'm told she makes the best muffins in the world."

My cheeks heat up the way they always do whenever someone uses that particular compliment because obviously, that would be impossible to gauge. I mean, I'm sure *someone* in the world makes better muffins than me. Maybe.

Travis takes in my appearance. Today, I'm wearing normal Lucy-goes-to-church clothes. A denim skirt with a peasant blouse and my dark curly hair is pulled back in a low ponytail. More importantly, it's minus the lizard.

"We met yesterday at the rec center opening," I tell Jim. "I was the one who found Abby Delgado."

"Oh, yes, I heard about that. Poor woman. Terrible accident. Finding her must have been awful for you."

Travis observes my expression carefully. He still thinks

I'm hiding something. Which I am. I have to give him credit. He's more than just a broad set of shoulders and a firm chin.

"It was really hard on her little dog. Or rather, her brother's dog. Abby was dog sitting for him."

Poor Paco spent the night having nightmares. I know this because I let him sleep at the end of my bed (hence, the reason I had to take the Benadryl) and he kept twitching and making all kinds of noises. I hated leaving him alone this morning.

"Where is the dog, by the way?" Travis asks.

"He's with me."

"I was finally able to get ahold of Derrick Delgado yesterday evening. To tell him about his sister's death."

"How's he doing?" The words are no sooner out than I flinch. This is a horribly dumb question. If something ever happened to Sebastian, I'd be comatose with grief.

"He's handling it the way you'd expect. Under the circumstances."

Which doesn't tell me anything.

"Is he back in town?" I don't know Derrick, but I'd like to pay him a visit to tell him how sorry I am about his sister. And to give him his dog back, of course.

"According to him he never left town. He's been in Mexico Beach this whole time."

"I don't understand. Abby told me her brother was away and that's why she was dog sitting."

Travis looks me square in the eye and says, "Derrick Delgado swears he doesn't own a dog."

I'M CONFUSED. Why on earth would Abby lie about her brother owning Paco? And just as importantly, why didn't I pick up on that lie?

Probably because it was mixed in with the other lie about the dog's name and that's the lie I focused on. All I know is that if Paco doesn't belong to Derrick, then who does he belong to?

I swing by my place to pick up the dog, and we go to the Whispering Bay Animal Shelter. Lanie Miller manages the place. She's Dr. Nate's sister and a real hoot. She and her girlfriend, Dhara, are Bistro regulars.

I explain the Paco situation to Lanie.

"What a cute little dog. He's definitely a Chihuahua mix, but there's some terrier there too. You said Abby told you he belonged to her brother, but the brother denies it?"

"That's the official story. At least, according to Officer Fontaine."

"I met him a couple of days ago. He came in here looking for a dog. He's pretty cute."

"The dog?"

She snickers. "The man."

"Not my type."

Lanie smiles sympathetically. She's the other person that I've confided in about my feelings for Will. She thinks I should tell him, but if I do that and he doesn't feel the same way, it will ruin our friendship. And my friendship with Will means everything to me, so I can't take that risk.

"Obviously Travis Fontaine isn't my type either, but if I were into boys, I'd be all over all that one. You should have seen the way he was with the dogs. You can tell a lot about a person by how they treat an animal."

"He adopted a dog?"

"Not yet. He's looking for a specific breed. He's going to volunteer here a few hours a week."

"That's...nice of him." *I suppose.*

Lanie picks up a scanner and runs it over Paco's back. "He's been neutered. Let's see if he's been chipped. Mmmm... We're in luck." She heads over to a computer. "According to the records, he belongs to someone named Susan Van Dyke from Destin. Let me give her a call." She picks up the phone and dials.

Destin is a resort town about thirty miles away. How on earth did Abby end up with this dog?

"No answer," Lanie says. She leaves a message with information on how to contact her. Lanie rubs Paco behind the ears, and he practically melts in her hand. "Hopefully, his owner will call back soon. But in the meantime, little guy, what do you say? Want to stay here and play?"

"Stay here?"

"Sure. I mean, you can't take him, on account of your allergies. Right?"

"Right." Last night was miserable. I could keep taking the Benadryl, but I hate how groggy it makes me feel.

"Heard anything from *Muffin Wars*?" Lanie asks.

"Not yet."

"You will. No one makes muffins the way you do." She puts a leash on Paco. "Say good-bye to Lucy, Paco."

"Are you sure he'll be okay? I mean, he's been traumatized. He was with Abby when she...you know, died. Is there a pet psychologist that can come see him?"

Lanie tries to hide her smile. "Don't worry. He'll be fine." She takes a long look at Paco. "I don't know anyone named Susan Van Dyke, but now that I look at him more closely, I swear I've seen this dog before. I'm just not sure where."

"If he needs anything, anything at all just let me know." I wave to him one last time. He looks at me with the saddest eyes. I hope he doesn't think I don't want him. I don't know a lot about dogs, but I can tell he's special. Regardless of Officer Fontaine's skepticism, Paco *did* lead me to find Abby's body.

CHAPTER SIX

EVERY MONDAY THE "TOP PEOPLE" as they call themselves from the Sunshine Ghost Society meet at The Bistro for breakfast. Phoebe Van Cleave is the first to arrive. It occurs to me that I never saw Phoebe or anyone else from the society after Abby's body was discovered, so I never got a chance to offer my condolences.

I hand her a coffee. "I'm so sorry for your loss. How is the group taking Abby's death?"

"Even though it's just been a couple of days, we all miss her something fierce. She was a valuable member of our society, you know."

The little hairs on my neck rise.

Phoebe isn't going to miss Abby one bit.

Betty Jean told me that Abby and Phoebe were involved in a power struggle within the group. With Abby gone, it looks like Phoebe's position is no longer in jeopardy.

"Do you know when her service is going to be held?" I ask.

"It's all up to the brother. Apparently, he's a real loser, but he was her only living relative, so he's in charge now." She hesitates. "You know, Lucy, there are all sorts of rumors circulating about Abby and a dog. Do you know anything about it?"

Oh boy. The little hairs on my neck are practically dancing now. I'm surprised Phoebe's nose hasn't gotten longer just standing here talking to me.

This last statement of hers is a blatant lie in that she most *definitely* knows something about Paco. And it's a whole lot of something too. The stronger my physical reaction, the bigger the lie.

But I can't very well call her out on it without exposing my gift. I'd love to find out more about Paco, so I'm forced to tell her what I know in hopes that maybe I can glean more info from her.

"The dog is a Chihuahua mix. Abby brought him here to The Bistro on Friday and told everyone that he belonged to her brother, but he denies the dog is his. The dog was with her when she died."

"Do you know where the dog is now?"

"He's at the animal shelter. Lanie Miller is trying to find out who owned him previously. In case they want him back."

"I've always wanted a dog. As Abby's dear friend, I should offer to adopt him."

Oh, hell to the no. Paco is such a smart little thing. He

belongs with someone hipper and let's face it, saner than Phoebe Van Cleave.

I make a mental note to call Lanie and tell that under *no* circumstances is Paco to end up with Phoebe. Before I can quiz her further on the subject of Paco, Gloria and Victor join us.

"Lucy, how have you been, dear?" Gloria's blonde hair is braided down her back today. She's younger than the rest of her group, but she's got streaks of gray in her hair that make her look older than thirty-nine (I asked her age once). If she cut and colored it, she'd probably look great, but then who am I to be giving out beauty advice? I can barely tweeze my eyebrows.

"I'm fine," I say automatically.

Gloria turns to Phoebe. "Have you asked her yet?"

Phoebe suddenly looks nervous. "Not yet."

Gloria reaches across the counter to take my hand in hers. "You know, Lucy, you don't have to pretend with us."

"O-kay. Not pretending, but if I was, what would I be pretending about?"

"When you find a dead body, you become linked to it."

"The spirit needs a conduit to hang on to," says Victor. "Chances are, Abby's spirit is hanging on to you."

"Have you felt different since Saturday?" Gloria asks. She eyes me curiously, and I can't help but feel creeped out. "We're expecting Abby to make an appearance any day now. She's the first of our group to go over to the other side. I'm hoping she can tell us what happened to her."

Oh, for Pete's sake. These wackadoos think that Abby is going to communicate with them through *me?*

I snatch my hand away. "Nope. I don't feel different at all."

"It's just a matter of time before you do. When it happens, you'll need us." Gloria slips me her business card. It reads **Gloria Hightower, Professional Medium**. "Call anytime. Day or night. If I'm not available, then leave a message."

Victor nods eagerly.

The whole thing is ghoulish. None of them are even sad that Abby has passed. It's as if they like her more now that she's potentially a ghost than when she was alive. How messed up is that?

Thankfully, Sarah comes along and saves me by getting their orders. Which means I take the next customer in line.

It's Rusty. And Travis is with him.

"Morning, Lucy!" says Rusty. "You know what I want."

I hand Rusty his usual—coffee heavy on the cream and sugar and a lemon poppy seed muffin.

"What'll you have, Officer Fontaine?"

"Just coffee. Black. And call me Travis."

"Are you sure you don't want something to eat? Our muffin of the day is pumpkin spice. First one's on the house."

"No, thanks. I'm more of a donut guy."

I knew it! "Then you should try Heidi's Bakery on Main Street. She makes great donuts, and her coffee isn't bad either."

"Thanks. I'll give it a try." Apparently, Officer Clueless doesn't understand sarcasm. "I checked in on Paco this morning," he adds.

This gets my full attention. "How's he doing?"

"He seemed to be doing fine."

Fine? That could mean anything. "Was he eating? How about the shaking?"

"He wasn't shaking."

He doesn't add anything else, so I give him his coffee. "Do you know when Derrick is planning on holding Abby's service?"

"Can't have the service till they finish the autopsy," says Rusty.

"*Autopsy?*"

"It's standard procedure whenever the cause of death is yet to be determined. But between you and me, it looks like that knock on the head did her in."

"What do you think happened? I mean, did she trip or something?"

"Or *something* might be more like it," Rusty says ominously.

Travis looks as if he's about to admonish Rusty when Betty Jean spies him from across the café. Her ability to sniff out testosterone never fails to impress me. She nearly plows down a mother and her toddler in her hurry to get to him. "You must be the new cop in town," she says breathlessly. "I'm Betty Jean Collins."

Travis shakes her hand. "Nice to meet you, Ms. Collins."

"Call me Betty Jean. Or better yet, Sugar Momma. Whichever you prefer. No one told me you were Ryan Reynolds' doppelganger. Ever see that movie *The Proposal*? I could have played the Betty White role, except she's a lot older than me. A *lot*. My favorite scene is the one where Ryan Reynolds catches Sandra Bullock coming out of the shower, and they end up on the floor naked. You can see his butt, and let me tell you, it's mighty fine. If you pause it, you can even—"

"I haven't seen the movie." Travis looks at me with desperation like he needs to be saved, but I'm enjoying this way too much to help him out here.

Betty Jean looks Travis up and down, then growls. "I guess it's true what they say about Texas. Is *all* of you this big?"

"Ah, Betty Jean, cut it out," says Rusty. "Or he'll think you're serious." Rusty playfully elbows Travis. "Betty Jean is like this with all the cops in town."

"No, I'm not. Just the good-looking ones I want to schnocker." She winks and saunters away. Even though I don't think schnocker is a real word, we all know *exactly* what Betty Jean means. The mental picture those words create in my head is more than a little disturbing.

Travis is left with his mouth hanging open.

Welcome to Whispering Bay, Officer Fontaine!

He shakes his head as if to clear it (he must have gotten the same picture I did). "Miss McGuffin, can we speak to you please? In private?"

Rusty makes a face. "Now? But I haven't eaten my muffin yet."

Travis looks at Rusty for a full three seconds like he's patiently counting to himself before saying, "Go ahead and have your breakfast. I can talk to Miss McGuffin."

"Gee, thanks!" Rusty happily takes off for an empty table near the window.

What on earth could Travis Fontaine want to speak to me about? I'm curious, but my Spidey sense warns me that the last thing I should do is go off for a private word with this guy.

"If this has to do with Abby, I told you everything the other day. Plus, I'm kind of busy. Working? You know?"

Sarah, who's just finished serving table three, overhears the last part of our conversation. "Go ahead, Lucy, Jill's in the kitchen, and I can handle the counter." She smiles at Travis who smiles back at her.

It's the first time I've seen him smile and... I hate to admit it, but Betty Jean is right. He does look like Ryan Reynolds. Sarah probably thinks she's doing me a favor. If only she knew how annoying he is.

It looks as if I have no choice but to talk to him.

"If you want to talk in private, then we should go upstairs."

CHAPTER SEVEN

THE UPSTAIRS APARTMENT was built by The Bistro's former owners, and it's completely awesome. Dark hardwood floors, creamy colored baseboards, and light gray walls give the place an upscale feel not to mention the breathtaking views of the gulf. I'd feel guilty living here, but Sarah and her husband also live on the beach in a renovated cottage, so it only made sense for me to take this place.

I can tell by Travis's expression that he's impressed. "Does every room up here have a view like this?"

"Yep. Except for the bathroom. The window in there looks out over the back parking lot, but I'm not complaining."

He changes gears and gets down to business. "Miss McGuffin," he says, and I swear I can hear Mrs. Jackson's voice from all those years ago in kindergarten, "I asked you if Miss Delgado seemed agitated last Friday and you said no, however, witnesses claim that the two of you had some words over a tuna salad sandwich."

"*Witnesses*? Who have you been talking to?"

He pulls out that notebook of his. "Gus Pappas, Viola Pantini—"

"Okay, okay." I blow out a breath. "I get it."

I should never have underestimated this guy.

"Sure, Abby and I had a few words, but it was nothing."

"It didn't sound like nothing."

"The tuna salad sandwich ruse is a little game Abby plays about once a month to get a free lunch. She orders it, then when I bring it out to her, she claims that I got the order wrong. Then I bring her what she really wants, a roast beef on rye and we give it to her for free."

"If you know that she's just yanking your chain, then why go along with it? Why not call her out on it?"

"Because I don't want to accuse her of lying."

"How do you know it's a lie? Maybe she's just forgetful."

"Oh, it's a lie, because—" I snap my mouth shut.

"Because what?"

Rats.

"You're right, maybe she has dementia." I try to sound meek even though it's killing me, but the last thing I want to do is admit my gift to Officer Fontaine. "I give her a free sandwich because I don't want to embarrass her and because other than the sandwich game, she's a good customer. Or rather, she *was* a good customer."

I shudder. I still can't believe she's gone. Poor Abby. What she was doing all alone in the rec center?

It's been two days, but I can still see it all so clearly. Abby, lying on the ground like she's asleep, wearing her tan skirt with sensible shoes...

Wait again.

My brain zeroes in on something.

Abby was wearing a tan skirt, sweater, and her brown loafers. It's a variation of what she wears most days when it's cool outside. But she specifically told me that she was going to be dressed as Annette Funicello.

So why wasn't she in costume?

The answer is obvious. I remember feeling her skin. She was cold and stiff. As if she'd been there a while...

Travis's voice cuts through my thoughts. "But last Friday, you did challenge her."

"What?"

"The tuna salad sandwich?" he prompts.

"Oh, right. I was tired. I'd been up late baking, and I was little friskier than usual." *Now it's my turn to ask questions.* "Why all this interest in what happened Friday? Have you figured out what Abby was doing in the rec center? Did she get in through the side door? Did you dust it for prints? Remember, you're going to find mine there."

"First things first." Travis flips through the pages in his notebook until he finds what he's looking for. "On the day of the rec center celebration you and Sarah Powers were working in your food booth, and according to Mrs. Powers,

Will Cunningham and your brother Sebastian came by around ten-thirty?"

That's Father McGuffin to you, buddy.

"That's right."

"But your brother wandered off, leaving Will and Brittany Kelly at the booth with you and Sarah Powers for about, what? Twenty minutes or so before you decided to go back into the building? And that's when you found the dog?"

"I already told you this at least four times the other day. And my brother didn't wander off. He and your dad went to go check out the rest of the food booths."

"Did you see him later?"

"Who? Sebastian or your father?"

"Sebastian."

"No. He probably got called away by a parishioner or something."

What's he trying to get at?

"Let's go back to Friday at lunch. Viola Pantini has gone on record as saying that Miss Delgado and Sebastian seemed at odds with one another. Something about an exorcism she wanted him to perform?"

I swallow hard. "I don't remember that."

"Gus Pappas also recalled an exchange between the two of them and it's very similar to Ms. Pantini's version. Apparently, Miss Delgado threatened to go to the bishop?"

"It was lunchtime, and we were busy, so I really can't... *Hold on*. You don't think Sebastian had anything to do with Abby's death? Just because she was upset with him on

Friday and then you're not sure where he was on Saturday during the celebration? Are you *insane*? Did you ask my brother where he was?"

"He says he was hearing a confession, but he won't tell us whose it was."

"You should know he can't tell you that. Besides, Abby wasn't killed during the rec center celebration. She died on Friday night or possibly early Saturday morning before the celebration began."

"How do you know that?"

"It's simple. Abby told me on Friday that she was going to be dressed as Annette Funicello, but she wasn't wearing a costume, which means she never went to the celebration. Plus, her body was cold. I mean, like really cold and stiff. I just didn't put it together until now."

A flicker of admiration flashes across his face. Have I actually managed to impress Officer Know-It-All?

"You're right. The coroner puts her time of death between midnight and two a.m. According to the security footage, Abby entered the building around midnight, but she never came out."

Security footage? I had no idea there were cameras around the building. Then I remember that Gus mentioned something about security issues.

"And your brother was seen entering the building thirty minutes later," Travis adds.

"My brother? Are you sure about that?"

"Positive. He even admits to it. Only he refuses to tell us what he was doing at the rec center in the middle of the night. He only says he saw Abby, stayed in the building a few minutes, then left."

"Okay, well, there you go. He was probably counseling her."

"In under five minutes? Maybe. Except the footage doesn't show anyone else entering or leaving the building. Which means that Sebastian is the last person who saw Abby alive."

The little hairs on my neck start to dance.

Is Officer Fontaine lying to me? I study him closer. His last statement wasn't exactly a lie, but it wasn't the complete truth either. He's hiding something from me, only I'm not sure what purpose it serves.

"I thought Rusty said she fell. Do the police think someone *killed* her?"

"I never said that," Travis says cautiously. "But we need Sebastian to tell us exactly what happened and we're hoping that you can convince him to do that."

"Well, I'll certainly try."

"Can you talk to him today? It's important we wrap this up as soon as possible."

I nod woodenly because even though I've just told him I'll try, I doubt Sebastian will tell me anything. Not if he feels that it will somehow betray a confidence.

I wait till Travis leaves, then I slump into my living room couch. My head is spinning. What on earth was Sebastian doing in the rec center in the middle of the night with Abby Delgado?

Even though a part of me knows it's irrational to blame

Travis Fontaine for any of this, I still can't help it. He might not have said it aloud, but he not-so-tactfully accused Sebastian of...who knows what?

As if my brother, the priest, who's never even hurt a fly in his whole life, was guilty of some kind of wrongdoing!

I grab a sweater and my car keys.

This situation calls for immediate action.

CHAPTER EIGHT

I EXPLAIN EVERYTHING TO SARAH, and since Jill has clean-up duty, she tells me to take the rest of the day off. I don't bother calling my brother because I don't want him to find an excuse to avoid me, so I charge over to the rectory.

It takes Sebastian a few minutes to answer the door. He looks surprised to see me in the middle of the day. "What's going on? Are you okay?"

I brush past him and plop myself down on the couch. "What on earth were you doing at the rec center in the middle of the night with Abby Delgado?"

"How did you—" He scrubs a hand down his face. "Never mind. So the cops came to see you, huh?"

"Yep. And I need you to fess up. Now."

He raises a brow at my use of the word "fess."

"Sebastian," I say trying to imitate our mother's voice.

"Okay. This is what I can tell you. Abby wanted me to perform an exorcism on someone she thought was possessed. I tried to humor her because she was a nice lady, and even though she belonged to that ghost society, she didn't have any real friends."

My shoulders sag. Abby wasn't one of my favorite people. Not even close. Most days she was a nuisance, but she was a loyal customer, and as kooky as it sounds, I'm going to miss her sneaky free lunch trick. It never occurred to me that she might have been lonely. I wish I'd been nicer to her that last day.

"Who did she think was possessed?"

"It's not relevant."

"Of course it's relevant! The police think that Abby's death wasn't accidental."

He stills. "They said that?"

"No one has to come out and tell me what's right under my nose. You should have seen that crew at the rec center. Taking pictures and fingerprints...and this Travis person running around like he's auditioning for the lead role in a *Law and Order* remake. So I'm going to ask you again. Who did Abby think was possessed? Let me guess, Phoebe Van Cleave?"

"All I'm going to tell you is that Abby had some concerns about a friend of hers and she wanted me to help. When I explained that I couldn't help in the way she wanted, then she became upset. Friday night she called and apologized for her behavior at The Bistro and asked me to meet her in the rec center. She said it was a matter of life or death."

"Didn't you think that was weird?"

"We're talking about Abby here."

"Point taken."

"So against my better judgment, I went. But when I got there, she told me that she didn't need me anymore and that everything had been taken care of."

"As in, taken care of because her friend was all right, or taken care of because she'd found someone else who'd perform her exorcism?"

"She didn't say, and frankly, I didn't ask because it was late and I was tired, and the whole thing was ridiculous."

Neither of us say anything for a few minutes.

"Okay, so you went to the rec center. You saw Abby. And the two of you talked."

He nods. "But don't ask me what we talked about, because that was confidential."

"You were there for about five minutes?"

"I wanted to walk her to her car, but she insisted on staying longer, so I left."

"And you never saw anyone else there?"

He hesitates like he's holding something back and I'm expecting his next words to be a lie. "Just the dog."

Hmmm.... Sebastian is telling the truth.

"One more question. Why did she want to meet inside the rec center? Why not here at the rectory? And how did you get inside the building?"

"That's two questions."

I give him the same look I use on Tony, our flour vendor, when he's late on his deliveries. I mean, how am I supposed to make muffins without flour?

It works because Sebastian answers, "I thought the rec center location was odd, not to mention illegal since we didn't have a right to meet there, but she was adamant. She said that since the building was haunted—her words, not mine—that it was the best location. She told me to go in through the side door. It was unlocked when I got there."

"You know they have security cameras? According to Travis Fontaine, you and Abby are the only ones who went into the building that night."

"That's what he told me."

"Sebastian, this all looks really bad."

"In what way?"

"In what way? If the police think that Abby was pushed or was involved in a struggle, then the fall that caused her death isn't accidental. And if you're the only person who was there that night... Do I really have to spell it out for you?"

"Are you saying that the police think I caused Abby's death?" He shuts his eyes for a few long seconds. "Dear God. They're right. This is all my fault. I should never have left her alone. I should have demanded that she allow me to walk her to her car."

"Oh no. You don't get to play the martyr. If someone did cause Abby's death, then that's on them. But don't you see? You have to tell me who she thought was possessed, because obviously whoever it was, might have had a motive to hurt Abby."

"I can tell you positively one hundred percent that the... person she thought was possessed didn't kill her."

"How can you be so sure?"

"Because I just am."

"And I thought I was the stubborn one in the family," I mutter.

"Why don't we let the police do their jobs? If anything sinister happened, then the truth will come out eventually."

"Eventually? You're so trusting of everyone. Zeke, sure, he's on our side. But this new guy? You should have seen the gleam in his eyes. He's practically feral."

"I think you've been watching too many episodes of *America's Most Vicious Criminals.*"

"And you haven't seen enough of them. You should see how wonky the evidence can be in these cases! There's plenty of innocent people who've been railroaded by the police, believe you me."

"Lu-cy," he says, mimicking Ricky Ricardo from the old *I Love Lucy* series. "Do you know something I don't?"

Usually, this makes me laugh, but not today.

"I know that Travis Fontaine has it out for you. What? Did you make him say too many Hail Mary's as penance on his last confession?"

Sebastian grunts. "First off, I never give out Hail Mary's as penance. That's old school. And it's called reconciliation now, which you would know if you ever went."

"I go. Sometimes. Just not to you. Now don't change the subject." I decide to pull out the big guns. "I should call mom and dad and tell them what's going on. I bet Mom could make you tell the cops what they want to know."

Sebastian gives me a look that makes me shrink into the

sofa. "Don't you dare ruin mom and dad's last week at the cabin."

I have to hand it to my big brother. He probably graduated top of his class in Guilt Infliction 101.

Our parents are what we call reverse snowbirds. After a lifetime of living in the Florida heat and humidity, they bought a cabin in Maine where they spend the summer months. They'll be back home in Whispering Bay sometime next week. Probably just in time to see Sebastian arrested.

He gets up from his chair. "Look, neither of us is going to change the other one's mind, so I suggest we get back to our lives and let our tax money be put to good use. Let the cops take care of it. Now, I have a sermon to work on. See you later, Lucy," he says back in Ricky Ricardo mode.

I go to leave, because what else can I do?

"By the way," he says casually in a way that makes me think he doesn't want to bring this up but feels like he has to, "have you spoken to Will lately?"

"Not since the day of the rec center celebration. Why?"

"It's just that he and Brittany are going out Friday night. On a date."

My stomach suddenly turns queasy, like I've licked too much raw muffin batter off the spoon (yes, I know it's not good for me but don't judge till you've tried it). This isn't exactly a surprise. Will told me he was going to ask Brittany out. But I must have been hoping that she'd turn him down.

And if that's the case, what kind of friend am I?

I do my best to smile. "That's great! I hope they have a good time."

"Lucy," my brother says gently, "Brittany's not a bad person."

Et tu, Sebastian? Those are the exact same words Will used to describe her.

Technically, I suppose it's true since as far as I know she hasn't been involved in any criminal activity since kindergarten.

"I'm sure you're right." Before he can say anything else, I kiss him goodbye on the cheek.

He gives me a smile meant to reassure me, but it's strained. Whatever happened between Sebastian and Abby has him troubled. He waits by the door until I get in my car and drive off. I might not be able to save Will from Brittany's French manicured clutches, but I can certainly do something to help my brother.

Let the cops take care of things?

Poor innocent, gullible Sebastian.

If he won't help himself out of this mess, then I'll have to do it for him.

Which means it's up to me to figure out what really happened to Abby Delgado.

CHAPTER NINE

MEXICO BEACH IS about an hour away, so it's after five by the time I get there. Our beautiful cool November weather has fizzled, and it's back into the upper eighties again. I'm hungry, thirsty and hot, but I'm on a mission.

I'm going to visit Abby's brother Derrick and offer him my condolences, which is the decent thing to do. Plus, I want to see if he knows anything about Paco. Just because Officer Fontaine says that Derrick denied owning the dog doesn't mean I should just take his word for it.

Since I'm assuming he's around the same age Abby was, I keep my fingers crossed that he still has a land-line which would mean he's listed in the phone book. But finding a phone book these days is like coming across a winning lottery ticket just lying around on the floor.

After three gas stations, I find one that still has a pay phone and I'm in luck. There's only one Derrick Delgado in the directory, and according to the map app on my smart-phone, his address is just a few miles away.

Mexico Beach is one of those communities on the gulf with the picturesque pastel houses, but Derrick's home is nothing like those. His trailer sits on the edge of town on a big isolated lot. The grass is overgrown, and there's trash strewn all over the place. I carefully make my way through the weeds, lest I accidentally step on a snake, because that would totally ruin my day. I should probably have called first, but my Spidey sense told me not to.

I walk up the wooden steps to the rickety porch and knock on the door. After a couple of minutes of nothing, I ring the doorbell for good measure just in case Derrick is hard of hearing. I wait for another couple of minutes, then give up. He must not be home.

I consider leaving him a note, when a man's voice says, "Turn around. Nice and slow and keep your hands where I can see 'em."

Definitely not words you want to hear when you're all alone out in the middle of nowhere. I gulp and turn around to find myself looking down the barrel of a shotgun.

But worse than that, sitting on the porch ledge next to the man with the shotgun, is a squirrel. And it's staring at me with his beady little eyes like he's ready to attack.

Most people find squirrels adorable, but they've been fooled. To me, squirrels are nothing more than aggressive rats with furry tails.

"Who the hell are you and what are you doing here?" The man is a little older than Abby was with a gleaming bald head and small brown eyes. His long-sleeved shirt is sweat-stained and stretched against a massive beer belly.

"Please, um, Mr. Delgado? I mean, I assume you must be Mr. Delgado, I don't mean any harm. Can you...can you tell your squirrel to go away?"

"My *what*?"

While still keeping my hands up, I gesture to the monster on the ledge. "Chip, Dale, Killer...whatever you call him. He's kind of freaking me out."

He snickers, then playfully aims the gun at the squirrel, who immediately takes off running across the lawn.

I breathe a massive sigh of relief. "Thank you!"

He turns the gun back on me. "What are you doing sneaking up on my house? Trying to break in?"

"No, of course not! I'm—"

"You from the bank?" The gun stays firmly aimed at my head, so I keep my hands in the air because I really don't want this bozo to shoot me.

"The *bank*? No, no... You have it all wrong. I was a friend of your sister's."

He relaxes a little. "If you're here to ask for something of hers so you can conjure her back up or whatever it is you people do, then you can forget it."

"You think I'm a member of the Sunshine Ghost Society?"

"If you were a friend of Abby's then you were definitely in that spook club of hers. Abby didn't have any other friends."

"I was more of an... acquaintance. Honest. I don't even

believe in ghosts. As a matter of fact, I laughed all the way through *Beetlejuice*."

"So you ain't one of those wackos?"

"Nope. I'm completely normal." *Sort of.*

"Then how did you know my sister?" He inspects me closer. Jeans, T-shirt, sneakers and a ponytail. Not exactly threatening attire.

"She was a customer," I squeak.

He lowers his gun. *Finally*!

"Why didn't you say so?" he grumbles. "I've been waiting for you all day."

"You have?"

"Sure. When the law office said they were sending a courier, I was expectin' a guy, but I guess these days that's politically incorrect or whatever bullshit you want to call it."

Law office?

I know I should identify myself immediately. I came over here today to tell Derrick how sorry I was about his sister, and to see if he knew anything about Paco, but as far as I'm concerned, this little Hee-Haw routine of his changes everything. Plus, I'd really like to find out more about this law firm business.

He walks around me and opens the door. "Let's get this over with."

If this were a scene from a movie, I'd definitely have blonde hair and big boobs. Because as foolish as it seems, I'm going to be the too-stupid-to-live heroine and follow a strange man who've I've just lied to and who seconds ago was pointing a gun at my head into his house.

Derrick Delgado's home is furnished moderately and is relatively clean compared to the outside. His T.V. is one of those old behemoths encased in a faux wooden box. Either he:

A) doesn't believe in flat screens.

B) can't afford to update.

Or

C) is afraid of plasma rays stealing whatever brain cells he has left.

I opt for B with a strong possible side of C.

He sits down on a beat-up sofa. I select the chair farthest from him. "I'm really sorry about your sister. Her death must have come as a shock to you."

"Sort of."

He watches me with an expectant gaze that makes me squirm. Or maybe the chair has a flea infestation. Or worse...

Concentrate, Lucy.

It's a total long shot, but maybe there's a chance he knew something about the exorcism. "Did you know that Abby was, um, being counseled by a local priest?"

"She wasn't religious. Unless you call that ghost society she runs around with a religion. More of a cult, if you ask me." He growls under his breath. "Don't tell me she left all her money to the Church."

Boy, this guy is a piece of work all right. His sister hasn't even been buried yet, and all he's worried about is that she might have left him out of her will.

Which means...

My heart begins to race. Then my cell phone goes off.

I glance at the screen.

Rats. It's Travis. This is the second time he's called in the last hour. The first time he left a message asking if I'd had a chance to talk to Sebastian. There's no way I'm going to tell him that I struck out with my own brother. Plus, I'm busy now. *Go away, Officer Fontaine.* I almost wish he could see the grin on my face as I hit the decline button on his call.

"Sorry about that. Now, where we were? Oh, yes, the will. I'm just a messenger so I'm not privy to the contents of Miss Delgado's will, but I heard that she had some dealings with a Father McGuffin from St. Perpetua's in Whispering Bay."

Wow. Not bad if I do say so myself. I'm actually pretty good at making things up on the fly.

"What the hell does that have to do with anything?"

"Nothing. I was just wondering if you wanted him to do the funeral service."

"Nah. I'm just going to have her cremated. Cheapest way to go and she won't care anyway. But I can't do that till they finish the autopsy. At least, that's what the cops told me."

"The police were here?" I ask, knowing full well that Travis has already spoken to him. But now I have to wonder if Travis asked Derrick where he was at the time of Abby's death, because I for one, would sure like to know.

"They were the ones who told me about Abby slipping

and hitting her head. Asked me about a dog, too, but I don't nothing about no dog."

My neck feels like it's been plugged into an electric socket.

I've just caught Derrick Delgado in a whopper.

"Why did they want to know about a dog?" I ask trying to sound innocent.

He scowls. "What do you care? Where are those papers you brought me?"

I rifle through my bag, pretending to look for them. "You're not going to believe this, but, um, I forgot the papers."

He rolls his eyes in disgust. "What's wrong with you people? First, you never return my calls. Now you show up here with no papers? Wouldn't have happened if they'd sent a man."

"I'll see if I can rustle you up one of those," I mutter.

He raises a bushy brow at me.

I clear my throat. "No worries. We'll get those papers back out here pronto."

"You better. Or I'll sue your firm for being a bunch of idiots."

CHAPTER TEN

AFTER MY VISIT to Derrick Delgado, I need to blow off some adrenaline, so I go to Will's house. He owns his own home, a cute little one-story bungalow a few blocks from the beach. The living room is minimalistic—just a couple of dark leather couches, a coffee table, a desk, and two big bookshelves overflowing with classic literature.

Will is a reading snob, preferring the classics to popular fiction. He's the only person I know who doesn't own a T.V. That's why we have to watch *America's Most Vicious Criminals* at my place.

I pace around the room and tell him everything I know so far about Abby's death, including the stuff about the video of Sebastian and Abby going into the rec center and my futile attempt to knock some sense into my brother.

"Sebastian refuses to tell me who Abby wanted the exorcism performed on. Only my money lands on Phoebe Van Cleave."

Will ponders this over. "Go on."

"According to Officer Fontaine, Paco doesn't belong to Derrick Delgado. So I went out to see him. He didn't know anything about a dog, but it was a big fat lie. You should meet this guy. He's like a character right out of *Deliverance*. Oh, and the worst part? The guy has a trained squirrel."

The corner of Will's mouth twitches up like he's going to laugh. Only he knows better.

When I turned seven, my parents threw me a pool party. My entire class was there (Mom's rules: everyone in the class is invited, or no one is). To keep him from being bored, Sebastian, who is five years older than me, was allowed to invite a friend, so he asked Will. And thank God for that because who knows what would have happened to me if Will hadn't been there to save me.

We'd just gotten out of the swimming pool. Mom had placed my ballerina cake with the seven pink candles on top of the picnic table, when out of nowhere, a pack of feral squirrels came flying out of the trees (Will and Sebastian like to say that it was only three, but honestly, when your life is flashing before your eyes, who takes the time to count?).

Those squirrels scurried toward my cake with every intention of stealing it.

No way was I going to let that happen, so I grabbed the cake and took off running. I could hear everyone shouting behind me, but all I could think about was those squirrels making off with my beautiful pink ballerina cake that Mom had baked from scratch.

I turned to see if the squirrels were following me (which they were!) when I tripped and began to fall. In one of those slow-motion clips of your life, I could see what would happen next. I was going to land face down on the patio tile, and worse, my cake would be ruined.

But then out of nowhere, a pair of arms grabbed me, holding me (and the cake) steady. "Get out of here, you grubby squirrels!" Will screamed.

Miraculously, they obeyed him.

By that time, Mom and Dad were also there to help. I didn't land on my face and break my nose. My cake was all in one piece. And the squirrels were vanquished back to their evil hiding nests.

If that wasn't a reason to fall in love with Will, (and hate squirrels forever), then I don't know what is.

I proceed to fill Will in about the rest of my visit to Derrick, omitting the part where he held a gun to my head, because if I tell him that he'll tell Sebastian and I don't want my brother to flip out. Plus, Sebastian would tell our parents, and then everyone would make a federal case about nothing.

Will crosses his arms over his chest. "The brother sounds like a nut job. I don't like it that you went out there to see this guy alone." *See what I mean?* Good thing I left out the part about the shotgun. "What's going to happen when he calls this law office and they deny knowing anything about you?"

"I never gave him my name, and I live an hour away. How's he going to find me?" Before Will can answer, I say,

"Don't worry about Derrick Delgado. We have more important fish to fry, like figuring out the cause of death. We won't
know anything more until the autopsy results come
back, but—"

"Wait." He sits up. "Are you saying that maybe Abby
was *murdered*?"

"Pay attention, Will! Why do you think the cops questioned Sebastian about what he and Abby were doing in the
rec center? They didn't come right out and say the M word,
but you should see the way this Officer Fontaine character
is acting. Someone needs to remind him he's not in Dallas
anymore."

"Sounds like you don't like Travis."

"He's a *donut* man."

Will chuckles. "He joined my basketball league last
night. He's got an awesome three-point shot."

All of which means that Travis has completely won
Will over because Will goes nutso over basketball. Personally, I've never gotten into the game. It's run down and make
a basket, then, run down and make another basket. Wash.
Rinse. Repeat. *Yawn.*

I stop pacing and glance around the room. It's suddenly
occurred to me that something isn't right. Will's usually
neat desk is cluttered with papers, and there's an empty
carton of Chinese on the floor next to his trash can like he
went to toss it in and missed. Will is obsessively neat. It's his
only fault.

"Work been busy?"

"I've been off for a few days. Mini vacation."

On his days off Will goes entirely off grid. No Internet, no newspapers, minimal cell phone contact. He says it helps keep him sane, but it would drive me bananas because I happen to like being around people. I wonder how Brittany would handle that if she and Will ever got together.

Before I can inquire why his desk is so messy, he asks, "Are you sure you can't get Sebastian to tell you anything more about that night?"

"He's stubborn as a goat. He refuses to help himself in anyway. But that's okay because I plan to solve this thing on my own."

"How are you going to do that?"

I smile, which makes Will frown uneasily. "Lucy, what are you up to?"

"I haven't told you the best part yet."

"There's a *best* part here?"

"Phoebe Van Cleave also lied to me about knowing that Abby had a dog. Add that to the fact that I'm pretty sure she's who Abby wanted the exorcism performed on, it makes her look mighty suspicious. Right now, she and Derrick are my two prime suspects."

"*Suspects?* I think you've been inhaling too many muffin batter fumes."

I snort because that's actually pretty funny.

"Okay," he concedes, "Let's say Abby's death wasn't accidental. What motive did the brother have for killing her? Or Phoebe Van Cleave for that matter?"

"Derrick has the oldest motive known to man. I think he must be Abby's heir because he was worried about her will, so it's money. As for Phoebe, there was a rumor going around that Abby was challenging her for her position as head of the Sunshine Ghost Society. I'm not sure what role Paco has in all this, but he's involved too."

"The dog?"

I nod. "I think Abby dognapped him and Phoebe definitely knows something about it, but like I said, she's lying."

"And you're sure about that?"

Will knows about my gift, but like Sebastian, he doesn't know the extent of my talent. "Positive."

Will is quiet for a few minutes while he's trying to absorb everything I've just told him. Or maybe he's already figuring out how we can solve this thing together. He's so smart, and two heads are definitely—

"Luce, have you thought that maybe finding Abby's body has made you a little more sensitive to this whole situation?"

"What do you mean?"

"Think about it. You found her body, and she was a customer. Someone you saw probably two or three times a week. She might not have been a favorite of yours, but you liked her because you like everyone. Finding her dead like that must have been a huge shock. Maybe you have some form of PTSD here."

"Are you *serious*?"

"I'm just saying that it's perfectly normal for you to still be freaked out about everything. I think Sebastian is right. I think you ought to let the cops handle this."

"You think I'm *freaked out*? Sorry, but you must be

confusing me with Brittany." The minute I say it I wish I could take it back because it sounds mean and jealousy. "I'm sorry. That was petty."

He sighs. "I told you before, she's not that person from high school."

Even though Sebastian has already told me all about their date, I still want to hear it from Will. "So, did you ask her out?"

He looks at me warily. "I actually wanted to talk to you about that."

"Oh, like you want my permission? I thought we already went through this."

"I know we talked about it some the other day, but if you really dislike her, I'll break the date. You're my best friend, but more than that, you're the best judge of character I know. Be honest. What do you really think of her?"

Oh boy. Will has no idea. He's just handed me the perfect opportunity to shoot Brittany down forever.

A part of me would love to tell him exactly what I think of her.

But the way he's looking at me right now like he trusts me explicitly makes me stop and reconsider.

I have to look at this through someone else's eyes. Besides my parents, Sebastian and Will are the two people I love and trust most in this world. If they both think Brittany is okay, then maybe I'm the one with the problem.

The truth is, I can't be objective here.

It kills me to say this, but I have to. "You should definitely go out with Brittany. Who knows? She could be the one. Besides, you don't want to be a schmuck, do you? What kind of guy asks a girl out and then cancels? Anyway, it shouldn't matter what anyone else thinks. Only what *you* think."

"You're right," he says sheepishly.

"That goes without saying."

Boy, Meryl Streep has nothing on me. I should probably go ahead and book my front row seat at the next Academy Awards presentation.

"I hope you won't mind if we skip our Friday night pizza and T.V. routine again," he says. "It was the only night Brittany was free this week."

"No worries. I can experiment bake. I really need to get this mango coconut muffin recipe worked out. You know, in case they call from *Muffin Wars*."

"You mean when they call."

"Sure, right."

He walks me out to my car, but it feels awkward between us.

"Wear a blue shirt on your date," I say. "It makes your eyes look less shifty."

He laughs, but it's strained. "So... Luce, can you tell when *I'm* lying?"

"Every single time. So watch it, buddy," I say, adding this to all the other lies I've told today because if Will knew that he was the only person I've never caught in a lie, it would sound strange and somehow, he'd figure out how I feel about him.

He shakes his head as if he's not quite sure he believes

me and waves goodbye. I wave back and begin the short drive back to The Bistro.

It's dark, but I always leave the back light on. I put my key in the door and am about to unlock it when an all too familiar whimpering stops me cold.

I whip around to find Paco staring back at me, his tail wagging furiously.

CHAPTER ELEVEN

I CALL Lanie and tell her about my surprise visitor.

"Oh, my God, I'm so glad he's with you! Is he all right?"

"He's fine. But how did he get here?" With my cell phone tucked under my chin, I bend down to give Paco a bowl of water. He eagerly laps it up.

"One of my staff went to take the dogs out for the night, but when she put them back in their cages, she noticed Paco was missing, so she called me. We found a hole he must have dug under the fence. Nothing like this has ever happened before. It's lucky that he found his way to you." Lanie pauses. "Or maybe, luck has nothing to do with it. Maybe he was trying to get back to you specifically."

It's almost two miles from The Bistro to the animal shelter with several residential neighborhoods in between. The thought that Paco walked all this way in the dark just to find me is pretty out there. But then, I'm basically a human lie detector, which most people would scoff at, so I suppose anything is possible.

"You make him sound like he's Lassie," I joke.

"Maybe he is. Or maybe he's something even more. Remember when I told you that I thought I'd seen him before? It all came back to me tonight when we were out looking for him."

"Oh yeah?"

"It's a long story. And kind of kooky."

"Try me."

"Not over the phone. I'll be there in a few minutes."

LANIE HANDS me her cell phone where she's got her Facebook app opened to a picture of a dog that's the spitting image of Paco. "I thought he looked familiar, but I didn't make the connection until now. You remember I told you his owner's name was Susan Van Dyke? Susan is, or rather was, this eccentric millionaire who lived in Destin. She claimed that Cornelius—"

"*Wait*. Are you telling me that Paco's real name is *Cornelius*?"

Lanie grins. "Yep. Anyway, she claimed that Cornelius had special powers, so she used to hold séances in her house, that kind of stuff. She passed away last week."

Paco looks between Lanie and me like he's following our conversation. Which, I must admit, is kind of adorable.

"What kind of special powers?"

"She claimed he could commune with the dead."

"As in—" I make air quotes— "*I see dead people?*"

Lanie giggles. "Not sure if Paco, or rather, Cornelius, is familiar with the movie *The Sixth Sense*, but basically, yeah."

No wonder Phoebe was so interested in the dog. She thinks he can talk to the dead. It's yet another motive for Phoebe to get rid of Abby. I mentally shake my head. Not gonna go there. I basically told Will that I'd leave Abby's death to the police.

"What happened to Susan Van Dyke?" I ask.

"She had cancer. Do you think she left Cornelius to Abby?"

"It makes sense since Abby was a member of the Sunshine Ghost Society, but why did Abby lie and tell me his name is Paco? And that he belonged to her brother?"

"Your guess is as good as mine. All I can tell you is that this is Cornelius. See?" She points to the top of the phone screen. "He has his own Facebook page and everything."

Cornelius Van Dyke, Canine Ghost Whisperer.

"He's got over a hundred thousand likes!"

"Impressive, huh?"

I bring the phone screen down to Paco's eye level. "Is this you, little guy? Are you Cornelius?"

Paco barks and wags his tail.

Lanie pulls a leash from her backpack. "The attorney handling Susan Van Dyke's estate called me saying that they'd gotten my phone message. Apparently, Susan's sister just came down from New York. I'll call her tomorrow morning and tell her I have Cornelius. Now that Abby is gone maybe the family wants him back."

Paco looks at the leash in Lanie's hand, and his tail stops wagging. He runs and hides beneath a table in the restaurant.

"I've never had a dog run away from me before." Lanie sounds hurt, but instinctively I know that Paco's refusal to go with her isn't because he doesn't like her. It's just that... he likes me more.

"He can stay here tonight. I'll be happy to take him back to Susan's family tomorrow."

"Are you sure? What about your allergies?"

"Another night of Benadryl isn't going to kill me."

Lanie smiles. "Thanks, Lucy!"

"No problem." Lanie gives me the information on Susan Elliot and we say goodbye.

I kick off my sneakers and head into the kitchen. Paco follows me. I'm too wired up to sleep, so late night baking it is. Even though I still haven't heard back from *Muffin Wars*, I have to keep believing that they'll call. The prize for winning is ten thousand dollars which would go a long way to paying off what I owe Will.

Mango coconut muffin recipe: take four.

I finish putting a batch into the oven when there's a knock on the door to The Bistro. It's almost midnight, so I can't imagine who might be out there. Paco runs in a circle and barks happily like he's expecting something good to happen.

"Who is it, boy? Not a ghost, I hope." I giggle at my own silliness, because really? A canine ghost whisperer?

Still, I can tell that Paco (because I refuse to call him Cornelius) is an exceptional dog. He walked all the way from the animal shelter to The Bistro to find me. And he undoubtedly led me to Abby's body. I hope that whichever one of Susan's relatives ends up taking him appreciates just how awesome he is.

Through the large glass pane I see a Whispering Bay police cruiser parked in front and Travis Fontaine standing outside. He's wearing his uniform, and he's alone.

I unlock the door and swing it wide to face him. "This is twice in one day, Donut Boy. Maybe you can't read, but we're closed."

If he's offended by my hostility, he doesn't show it. He looks at Paco and frowns. "What's the dog doing here? I thought he was at the animal shelter."

"He ran away."

"And you found him?"

"More like he found me."

He looks at my bare feet, then his gaze slowly sweeps up to take in my jeans and T-shirt. I'm sure my hair has flour in it because I'm a little messy that way when I'm baking but it's better than a dead lizard.

I feel antsy under his perusal. "What are you doing here?"

"Your lights were on, and since I was planning on coming to talk to you first thing in the morning, I figured now was as good a time as any." He shrugs, and for the first time, he seems uncertain. Or maybe he realizes how late it is and he's embarrassed.

I usher him into the café. He glances at my empty coffee pot longingly, so I take pity on him and start up a fresh brew.

"Late night patrol?"

"Technically, I'm a rookie on this squad, so yeah, I'm catching all the crap hours."

He doesn't say anything else until the coffee is ready. I pour him a cup and make one for myself, and we migrate to a table in the front of the restaurant. Paco jumps on Travis's lap and instead of shooing him off, he playfully scratches him behind his ear while he takes a long appreciate sip of the coffee. "You remembered I take it black."

"I remember how all my customers like their coffee. If you're here about Sebastian, I couldn't get him to tell me what he was doing in the rec center with Abby."

"That's too bad. But that's only one of the reasons I stopped by. We got a call from the Mexico Beach Police Department to be on the lookout for a possible scam artist. Derrick Delgado called them with a complaint about a woman impersonating a member of the law office handling his sister's will."

"Really? Who would do that?" I don't even blink, I'm that good now. Who knew that lying was one of my many talents?

"He described her as mid-twenties with dark curly hair, big brown eyes, and glasses." He looks at me over the rim of his cup. "You know anyone who might fit that description?"

"Is that all we have to go on? I mean, that could be anyone."

"Apparently she's also afraid of squirrels."

"It's called scuirophobia, and it affects over two hundred and fifty thousand Americans."

He stares at me.

"I must have picked that up playing one of those kinky trivia games."

He continues to stare.

"Not that I have it! No way. I *love* squirrels. I'd have one as a pet if it didn't violate a health code or something."

"Mr. Delgado was also quite impressed by the way she was able to, as he put it, fill out a pair of jeans."

I almost choke on my coffee. "*Yuck!* He must be at least seventy years old!"

"Miss McGuffin, are you seriously going to tell me it wasn't you?"

There's no way I can fudge around this, so I confess. "Okay, it was me. And...call me Lucy." Which is only fair since this morning he asked me to call him by his first name. Plus, Miss McGuffin sounds ridiculous.

"What were you thinking?"

"I thought that I'd offer my condolences."

"So why lie to him and tell him you were from a law firm?"

"That was an accident."

"I bet."

"No, really, he just assumed that I was from the firm."

"And you didn't clear it up." It's a statement, but he wants to know the reason behind my actions.

The oven timer goes off. Talk about being saved by the bell.

"Hold on." I run back to the kitchen to pull the muffins out of the oven. When I turn around, Travis is standing in the doorway, which is a little offsetting. This kitchen is my private place, at least, at night it is. Even though it's a good sized room, he makes it seem small. And *warm*. Must be the heat from the oven.

"Do you always bake this late at night?"

"It's a new recipe I'm trying out for *Muffin Wars*."

He raises an amused brow.

"Get your mind out of the gutter. It's a television baking competition on the Cooking Channel. I sent in an audition tape, and I'm waiting to hear back."

"Whatever that is, it smells good."

"Too bad you don't like muffins, or I'd let you try one."

He leans back against the counter and watches as I putter around the kitchen. Paco raises his nose in the air and sniffs appreciatively.

"You," I say to Paco, "Can have whatever you want." He pants in anticipation.

"Weird. It's like he can understand you," Travis says.

Exactly. I mentally debate whether or not to tell him about the dog. Travis is a cop, and for whatever reason, Zeke seems to think highly of him. Maybe if I share everything I know he'll lay off Sebastian.

"Lanie Miller came to see me. The dog's real name is

Cornelius." I tell him all about Paco's famous persona and how I think Phoebe Van Cleave is somehow involved too.

"A canine ghost whisperer?" he says incredulously.

"Susan Van Dyke might have willed the dog to Abby after her death. But it doesn't explain why Abby told me the dog's name was Paco. Or why she told me he belonged to her brother." *Or why the brother lied to me about it.* But I can't tell him this last part without revealing my gift.

"Maybe Abby changed the dog's name. A lot of people do that. As for the lie about the brother owning the dog, I have no clue. Unless..."

"Unless the dog wasn't willed to her and maybe she stole him?" I finish.

"Could be."

"I'm taking the dog back to the family tomorrow. I guess I'll find out the truth then."

He glances at the muffins. "Is that coconut?"

"Mango coconut. But I haven't worked out all the kinks in the recipe yet."

I touch the top of a muffin, and it doesn't feel so hot anymore. Gingerly, I ease one out of the tin then cut it in half, let it cool off a bit, and offer it to Paco, who wolfs it down in two gulps.

"Looks like Cornelius approves."

"He's Paco," I automatically correct him. "At least while he's here with me. Cornelius is such a stuffy sounding name."

Travis stares at the other half of the muffin.

Nope. Don't even think about it. Officer Fontaine sealed

his culinary fate when he decreed himself a donut man.

"Any word on the autopsy report yet?" I ask.

"Not yet."

"But Abby died when she hit her head, right? Do you think someone knocked her down?"

"I can't discuss that with you."

"Look, you seriously don't think my brother had anything to do with her death. He's a priest, for God's sake."

"Your brother is hindering a police investigation by refusing to tell us what he and Abby were doing in the rec center in the middle of the night. There's also the matter of the unlocked door. Technically they're both guilty of trespassing."

"Well, gee, Abby's dead, so I guess that just leaves Sebastian to arrest. What? Are you trying to fill a quota or something?"

His jaw tightens. I can't help but feel a teeny bit sorry for him. He's basically stuck between a rock and a hard place. I begrudgingly hand him the other half of the muffin. "Try this. It'll make you feel better."

He eats it almost as fast as Paco did.

"This is really good."

"Did you think it wouldn't be?"

"No, I mean, it's *really* good."

"Why, Officer Fontaine, are you flirting with me?" The second I say it, we both freeze because *I'm* the one who sounds like she's flirting. "That didn't come out right." I pull another muffin out of the tin and hand it over like a peace offering. "Here. In case you get hungry later."

"Thanks." He takes it and says casually, "I told you, call me Travis."

Travis. It's a name for a lumberjack. Or an old-time western sheriff. It totally fits him.

"Did you ask Abby's brother where he was at the time of her death?"

He narrows his eyes.

Rats. I've just unwittingly reminded him about my nefarious visit to Derrick Delgado. "As a matter of fact, I did. He was playing cards with friends."

"And you checked up on that?"

"I have two people who swear Derrick was with them from midnight till two in the morning. Even if the time of death is off by an hour, it's impossible to make it from Mexico Beach that quickly. It's just too much of a stretch."

That all sounds logical enough.

Except I can't get the niggling feeling that of all people, Derrick had the most to gain by Abby's death. "I'd like to know why he's so anxious to get her will resolved."

"He's her next of kin. No husband. No kids."

"That's what I figured. If Abby has any money, I'm sure Derrick will be appreciative. He looks like he's pretty much living month to month."

Travis doesn't blink. Or say a word.

Which...tells me *everything*.

Holy wow. His face is an open book. Only, I'm pretty sure he hasn't moved a muscle. It's like I just know what he's thinking. A surge of excitement rushes through me. I've never been able to read *anyone* this easily.

"Abby was loaded, wasn't she?"

He frowns. "How did you know that?"

"Lucky guess?"

He shakes his head as if to clear it. "I should be getting back on patrol. Thanks for the coffee and the muffin."

"Right."

I follow him out of the kitchen and back through The Bistro. He stops at the front door and turns to look at me. Boy, he's tall. His green eyes still radiate snark, but there's something else there too. Something that makes me feel even warmer than when we were in the kitchen.

"Even though it was a bust, thanks for talking to Sebastian. But no more pretending to be someone else. Got it?"

"Got it." I mentally cross my fingers, because how on earth can I make a promise like that?

"And if you don't mind, can you let me know what happens tomorrow with the dog? I'd really like to know if Abby had a legit claim to him."

I bat my lashes at him. "Anything else I can do for you?"

Yikes, that sounded kind of flirty too. *What's wrong with me*? Maybe Will is right. Maybe I have been inhaling too much batter fume.

"As a matter of fact, there is something you can do," he says. "Make sure to lock your door."

"Sure, but you know, that's not really necessary. Whispering Bay is the safest city in America."

We both look at each other for a second, and in that tiny iota of time, I'm struck with the eerie realization that neither of us really believe that.

CHAPTER TWELVE

AFTER THE MORNING rush slows down, I call the number Lanie gave me for Susan Van Dyke's lawyer. He isn't available, so I give the receptionist my name and information and ask that he call me back as soon as possible. I have to admit, a part of me is relieved because I'm just not ready to give Paco up.

I don't think he's ready to give me up either. The little minx seems perfectly content in his new surroundings. Last night he slept in my bed again (I should probably nix that). He happily trots up and down the stairs between my apartment and The Bistro (the customers think he's adorable), and right now, he's napping on my living room couch like he doesn't have a care in the world.

Because I stayed up late baking and then had to take Benadryl to keep from itching, I feel like I'm dragging. Combined with the tension of the last few days, I think some exercise is in order. I decide to go to the new rec center and check out the classes.

It's the first time I've been in the building since the opening day celebration. After Abby's body was found the indoor facilities were sealed off for the rest of the day and the tours were rescheduled for Sunday with the center going operational on Monday. Today is Tuesday, and the place is packed.

I check in at the front desk and peruse the schedule. I'm an hour too late for Zumba and two hours too early for Brittany's Pilates class (not in the least bit sorry about that), but there's a yoga class for active and mature adults taught by Viola that starts in two minutes. It probably won't be much of a challenge, but it's better than nothing.

I sneak in through the back door to the room and grab a mat. The rest of the class is made up of the usual suspects— Betty Jean and Gus, Phoebe's brother Roger who co-owns the local paper and some more of the Gray Flamingos. Out of the corner of my eye, I see Jim Fontaine talking to Gus. I'm glad Jim is making friends.

Everyone looks at me curiously as if I'm in the wrong class. I'll have to tone it down some so that I don't stand out.

Viola waves to me from the front of the room. "Lucy! We're so happy to have you join us this afternoon."

"Thanks! Happy to be here!"

Viola proceeds to lead a dozen senior citizens and me through an hour of deep breathing, stretching and yoga-ass-kicking positions.

Even though I'm about four decades younger than the

average student, I'm the only one who's wheezing at the end of class.

Viola drapes a towel around her neck. Her skin is glowing with vibrant health. I, on the other hand, am sweating. Not perspiring, but drip-all-the-way-to-the-floor sweating like a construction worker in August.

It's embarrassing. Who knew that active and mature are really senior citizen code words for *really in shape*?

"How did you like the class?" Viola asks.

"It was great," I pant before taking a big swig of my bottled water.

"You're welcome to come back anytime," she says with a smile before going around to make small talk with the rest of the students.

Betty Jean slaps me on the back. "Look who's having a hard time keeping up with the old folks. Ha-Ha!"

I make a mental note to step up my cardio routine.

"Say, now that you're hanging out with the Geritol crowd, you should join our book club."

"Oh, well, um..."

"This month we're reading J.W. Quicksilver's newest thriller. Four people are assassinated in the opening scene. It's awesome."

"J. W. Quicksilver? I've never heard of her. Or is it a him?"

"It's a him, but that's definitely a pen name. He probably has one of those big top-secret state department jobs because he sure does seem to know a lot of hush hush stuff. And those sex scenes. Whew!" Betty Jean fans herself with her hand. "If he's done even half the stuff he writes about in his books, Mrs. Quicksilver is one lu-cky lady."

"Mmm... I'll think about it."

A really buff guy wearing a black T-shirt walks through the hallway and is immediately picked up by Betty Jean's radar. "There goes one of those yummy personal trainers! I need some help with the elliptical machine if you know what I mean. See you later, Lucy. And if you're interested in the book club, we're meeting next Thursday at my house. But don't drag your feet. You need to let me know ASAP because technically, there's a waiting list. But if you promise to bring muffins, I'll shoot your name up to the top." She sprints across the room to catch up to the trainer.

I stuff my water bottle back inside my workout bag and turn to leave when Jim comes over to say hi. "Good class, huh?"

"I'll be honest, I didn't think it would be this challenging."

His gaze lingers on Viola, who's still talking to a few of the ladies. "She really knows her stuff." The way Jim looks at her makes me nervous for him. I hope he realizes that Viola and Gus are an item. "Want to get a smoothie?" he asks. "My treat."

"Sounds good. Thanks."

The fresh juice bar is located near the back of the rec center and has an outdoor patio facing the water. Jim hands me my pineapple mango vitamin enhanced smoothie, and we sit at the lone empty table.

"How are you liking retirement?" I ask.

"More than I thought I would. There's always something that needs doing. And this new center is great. I signed up for a pottery class that Viola recommended."

I glance back toward the building, and my whole body involuntarily shivers.

He notices my reaction. "Are you all right?"

I don't have to ask what he means by that. "Will, that's my best friend, thinks I have PTSD."

"In my experience as a homicide detective, I've seen a lot of people go through a myriad of emotions when they encounter a dead person."

I tell Jim all about Abby's connection with Sebastian, the bit about Phoebe and Abby vying for control of the Sunshine Ghost Society, Paco, my visit to Derrick Delgado, everything. He's so easy to talk to it all just spills out. Every now and then he nods his head encouraging me to continue. I can see why he was such a good detective. He's the kind of person other people want to tell things.

"So what do you think?" I ask.

"I'm not a psychologist, but I don't think you have PTSD."

"Neither do I." We both smile. "Can I ask how you'd solve this case?"

"Well, like my son, I'd like to know what Abby was doing inside this building late at night. And I'd like to know who she wanted an exorcism performed on and why she lied about the dog. But unless Father Sebastian opens up..." His brow puckers in concern. "I'll be honest, Lucy, once that autopsy report comes back, I wouldn't be surprised if your brother is brought down to police headquarters for questioning."

"But he didn't do anything wrong!"

"Then he doesn't have anything to worry about."

"That's what he says, but you and I both know that if Abby told him anything in confidence, he won't reveal it."

He sighs. Maybe we'll never know exactly what happened. Maybe some cases just aren't meant to be solved."

"Like your Angel of Death case?" I ask softly.

"That case is one of the reasons I put off retirement. I wanted so badly to be able to look at the families of the victims in the eye and tell them that I'd caught their loved one's killer. But after all these years it's all gone cold."

"Weren't most of the victims terminally ill?"

His eyes harden. "Yes, but that didn't give her the right to take their lives."

"I agree." I don't want to bring up bad memories for him, but I really am curious, so I ask as delicately as possible, "What made the case so difficult to solve?"

"There were six known victims, but the FBI and my department think the number might have been almost double that. Most of the time the clue to finding a serial killer is the information we get from the first victim, and we simply don't know who he or she was."

Even though this is all a little ghoulish, I can't help but be fascinated.

"I watched the episode when it was featured on *Ameri-*

ca's *Most Vicious Criminals*, but I have to admit, I've forgotten the details."

"The first victim was probably someone important to her. A patient or family member she cared about and didn't want to see suffer anymore, so she slipped them a little extra morphine. Since the victim was probably very close to dying anyway, no one would have thought to do an autopsy or check their blood for the presence of excessive drugs."

It's coming back to me now. "The victims all died of narcotic overdoses, right?"

He nods. "Easy enough to do fifteen years ago when hospitals didn't have the kind of security measures they do now. She could have easily upped their dose through a drug pump and then recalibrated the machine back to the normal dose before anyone checked."

"But you do know that the murderer was a she?"

"The truth is, the murderer could be a man for all we know. The only thing I'm certain of is that he or she had enough medical knowledge to be able to manipulate a narcotics pump. They might have worked for the hospital, or one of the temp agencies, or hell...they could have even come in as a visitor. And it wasn't limited to one area of town. The murders occurred in multiple hospitals."

"What was the motive?"

"Most likely, in her delusional mind, she probably thought she was helping them. Unless we're lucky enough after all these years to catch a break in the case, we'll never know the exact motive. We interviewed hundreds of people, watched hours and hours of surveillance tapes, but we never had enough evidence to arrest anyone. Our *Angel,*" he says mocking the nickname, "was clever. We know very little about him or her."

"How do you even know it was the same person?"

He hesitates. "This was never released to the press or featured in the T.V. show, but our Angel left a note each time they struck."

I swallow hard. "What did it say?"

"R.I.P."

"Rest in Peace?"

"Yep. Always written in pencil on a paper towel from the victim's hospital room in block style letters."

I fidget with the straw on my drink. "In your experience, Jim, what would you say the number one motive for killing someone usually is?"

He shrugs. "Depends. Money, anger, jealousy, power. Every murder is unique."

"But money is a big one?"

"Oh yeah. It's straight out of the Detective 101 handbook. Follow the money trail and chances are, you'll find the killer."

Which would make Derrick Delgado the most logical suspect.

"Can I ask you a few questions? As a professional?"

Jim's green eyes sparkle with humor. "Shoot."

"According to Travis, Abby died sometime between midnight and two a.m. The surveillance cameras caught Sebastian leaving the building a little after twelve-thirty, and since he left Abby very much alive, that would narrow the time of death to sometime between twelve-thirty and two."

"Go on."

"Abby's brother, Derrick Delgado, is her heir, and according to Travis, she left him a bundle."

Jim's eyes narrow. "He told you that too?"

"Not in so many words. I sort of...inferred it."

No one except my family and Will knows that I'm a human lie detector. Not Lanie. Not Sarah. But what the heck. Like I said, Jim is really easy to talk to, but more than that, even though I barely know him, something deep in my gut tells me to trust him. If anyone will believe me, it's him.

I take a deep breath. "This might sound odd, but I can always tell when someone is lying. Or hiding something."

He doesn't say anything for a few seconds. "That must prove interesting."

"You think I'm strange."

"Not at all. I believe that some people are very adept at reading others."

"It's more than that. I can see through the most benign lies. Go ahead. Try and lie to me."

"You want me to lie to you?"

"In a way you already did. When you called my gift interesting when what you really meant was something else."

He grins sheepishly. "Okay, I'll play along. Let's see, I got married when I was twenty-four."

"That's the truth."

"My wife's name was Julie."

"True."

"Our anniversary is May thirteen."

"None of those were lies, Jim."

He frowns. "I made that too easy. Let's go again. This time I'll tell you three things in a row." He pauses to think. "Got it. Here you go: Travis's middle name is James." He pauses. "Julie was a schoolteacher." Another pause. "Our first home was on Spring Street."

"Your wife wasn't a schoolteacher."

He blinks. "What?"

"Your wife wasn't a teacher," I repeat.

"What made you pick that one?"

"All three statements were important to you because they're about your family. I can't explain it because it's different for everyone, but with you, there's a hitch in your voice when you talk about your family, but the bit about your late wife being a teacher, it was devoid of any emotion. Like it didn't matter to you because it wasn't real."

He looks stunned. "I thought I was careful to keep my voice the same."

I shrug.

"How long have you been able to do this?"

"Ever since I can remember. And, I'm kind of sensitive about it, so I'd appreciate it if you keep what I've just told you between us."

"Of course," he says, but I can tell he's still not sold. "Have you ever thought of going to Vegas? You'd make a killing at the poker tables."

I laugh. "Not my thing."

He raises a brow playfully. "You never know."

"So, back to Abby." I glance around the building. "Let's say someone wanted to get inside this building without being seen. How do you think they'd do it?"

"You mean how would they avoid the security cameras? From what I can tell, almost every door has one, so it would be almost impossible."

Not what I wanted to hear since according to Travis, the only people seen on tape entering the building that night were Abby and Sebastian.

He must sense my frustration because he gets up and tosses the rest of his avocado shake into a nearby trashcan. "Want to show me the door you came through?"

"For real?"

"Why not? I have to admit, Lucy, you've intrigued me."

We walk around to the side of the building. Everything appears the same as the day of the rec center opening, except this time the door is locked.

He glances up at the security camera, then back at the door. "The way the camera is angled, it would be impossible to get through this door without getting caught on tape. Except..." He looks at me. "What was the time frame on the security footage?"

"I'm not sure. I just know that Travis said that—wait. Are you saying that maybe someone came in this door *earlier* and was waiting inside the building? Gus told me on the day of the celebration that not everything was a hundred percent operational, including the security. At the time it didn't mean anything to me, but maybe he was talking about the cameras."

"It certainly sounds like something that should be checked out."

"So maybe Derrick snuck in the building earlier. He could have totally waited till Sebastian left. Maybe they argued, and he pushed her."

"Does he have an alibi for the time of Abby's death?"

"He claims to have been playing poker in Mexico Beach. And Travis said it checked out."

"Well, there you go. Sounds like the brother is off the hook."

As much as I hate to admit it, Jim is right. But I still can't shake the feeling that Derrick Delgado is hiding something big.

My cell phone pings. It's Susan Van Dyke's attorney. He tells me that technically the dog now belongs to Susan's sister, Deborah, so I make arrangements through him to drop Paco off at Susan's home this afternoon.

I thank Jim for the smoothie and the conversation and reluctantly head back to The Bistro. It's time to return Paco to his family.

CHAPTER THIRTEEN

SUSAN VAN DYKE'S home is in an upscale neighbor-
hood with a privacy gate. To get inside, I have to pick up a
security phone.

"Can I help you?" asks a crusty sounding male voice.

"This is Lucy McGuffin. I spoke to Ms. Van Dyke's
attorney about returning Pa—, I mean Cornelius."

The gate slowly opens which is my cue to come
through. As I guide my car into the circular driveway, the
house comes into view. It's a two-story red brick mansion
that seems out of place with the more coastal Mediter-
ranean architecture of the other homes on the street.

Paco and I get out of the car and are greeted by an older
gentleman wearing a black tie and jacket. It's like he's just
stepped off the set of *Downton Abbey*.

"I'm Anthony," he says, "Ms. Susan's former butler."

Paco barks and wags his tail. Anthony bends down and
pats him on the head affectionately. "Cornelius. It's so good

to see you, sir. And in such good health! I must say, this is a huge relief."

Sir? I try not to giggle. "So this is... I mean, this was Susan Van Dyke's dog?"

"Oh, yes, this is definitely our Cornelius. I'd recognize him anywhere."

Even though I'm glad that Paco is being reunited with his family, a part of me is sad too. Which is utterly selfish because it's not like I could adopt him myself.

Paco trots into the house like he owns it, which, I suppose, he kind of does.

"Miss Deborah is in the study." Anthony ushers me into a good-sized room filled with dark wooden shelves. A woman, maybe in her late seventies, thin and very fashionably dressed, is wrapping up books and placing them into a packing box.

Paco catches sight of her and freezes.

"I see the little mongrel has found his way back home." She studies me with cool blue eyes. "You must be Miss McGuffin. The lawyer said you would be by today. Let's get this over with. How much do you want?"

"I'm not sure what you mean."

"Aren't you looking for a reward for returning Cornelius?"

My spine stiffens. "No reward necessary. I just want to see him returned to his family."

"Unfortunately his family, as you put it, is dead."

"I'm sorry for your loss."

"Thank you." She goes back to packing up the books,

which I suppose is my cue to slink off, but there's no way I'm leaving Paco with this cold fish until I know for certain he'll be well taken care of.

"Does he belong to you now?"

"I live half the year in Manhattan and the other half in Paris. My lifestyle isn't suited for a dog."

I frown. "What sort of provisions did your sister make for Cornelius?"

"You mean, in her will?" She laughs like I've just said something funny. "Susan would never leave me her precious Cornelius. She knew how much I detested him. Unfortunately, my sister didn't make any provisions for the dog. I suppose it simply never occurred to her that the dog would outlive her. She was very egotistical that way."

"Oh. I thought...that is, I thought she had cancer."

"She did. But she'd been in remission for a while now. Her death came as a surprise." She narrows her eyes at me. "How did you end up with the dog?"

"He was a with a woman named Abby Delgado. Does that name ring a bell?"

"No, but I didn't know a lot of my sister's friends. Like I said, I don't live here. I just came down to clear up her estate and put the house up for sale."

"Abby, that's the woman who had Cornelius, died unexpectedly a few days ago. I'd assumed that Susan had given her the dog."

"I had no idea Florida was so dangerous," she deadpans. She looks down her nose at Paco. "Or perhaps you're the bad omen."

I *really* don't like this woman. Although, she has a point. How strange that both Susan and Abby died just days apart from one another. "Do know how Abby might have gotten possession of Cornelius?"

"A few days after Susan died, the little beast needed to go outside to do his business." She shudders in disgust. "Naturally I put him out in the yard to give him his privacy like I'd done before. Only this time, when I went to let him back inside, he was gone."

In other words, Deborah put him out, forgot all about him and Paco probably ran away. I catch Paco's gaze. I swear he's looking at her with the same disgust that I feel.

"Can I ask what you plan to do with him?"

"Find him a good home, I suppose." She looks at me with renewed interest. "Do you want him?"

"Absolutely."

With my allergy getting in the way, I can't keep him. But no way am I going to let Paco's fate rest in Cruella deVil's spiny fingers. I'll find him a good home of my own choosing. Maybe Lanie will take him.

"Wonderful. Anthony will show you and Cornelius out now."

She can't get rid of us fast enough which is just as well because (and I think I can speak for Paco) neither of us want to stay a minute longer than necessary.

I don't need anyone to show me out. I scoop Paco up in my arms, and just as I'm about to open the door on my own, Anthony shows up.

"I'm good—"

He motions with his hand for me to be quiet. "If you don't mind, miss," he whispers, waving me off to the side.

The butler wants a private word with me. The whole thing is deliciously creepy, so, naturally, I go along.

He guides me through a hallway that leads into a large kitchen. Compared to the rest of the house, which is dark and overly formal, this room is bright and sunny.

A middle-aged woman with caramel colored skin dressed in black pants and a white shirt breaks out into a smile at the sight of us. "Cornelius! I'm so glad you're back!" She bends down and scratches Paco behind the ears. "We've been so worried about you!"

I introduce myself to the woman. Her name is Aurelia. She's Anthony's wife and the cook for the estate. "You'll join us for tea?" She pours me a cup without waiting for my response.

It would be rude to decline, plus she's just set a yummy looking plate of scones in the center of the table. She gives Paco a scone and lays down a bowl of water for him.

I'm not a huge tea drinker, but the scones are delicious. I should probably get her recipe. "I love your accent. Jamaica?" I ask.

"Ya mon," Aurelia says, doing a Bob Marley imitation that makes me laugh. "How did Cornelius end up in your care?"

I tell them about Abby.

"How interesting," Anthony says carefully in a way that makes me think he wants to say more.

"How long did the two of you work for Ms. Van Dyke?"

"I've been with her for thirty years." He smiles tenderly at Aurelia. "And the missus here joined us almost fifteen years ago. I took one bite of her scones and fell instantly in love."

"I don't blame you."

Aurelia blushes prettily. "Susan was like family. We would take Cornelius ourselves, but now that the estate is going up for sale, we're planning to do some traveling. We're starting with a world cruise."

"A world cruise? That sounds fabulous. And, kind of expensive, huh?"

"Susan was very generous in her will," Aurelia says primly.

"She had cancer?" I ask.

Aurelia nods. "Yes, poor lamb." She makes the sign of the cross. "May her soul rest in peace."

"Her death still came as a bit of shock," says Anthony. "She'd been in remission for so long. Up till the end, she was very active with her charities and of course, with her special projects."

I have a pretty good idea just what those special projects might be.

"Was Susan involved with the Sunshine Ghost Society?" I ask delicately.

"Oh yes," Anthony says, "Susan was very involved with those kinds of groups. She used to host séances here at the house all the time. They came because of Cornelius. He's extremely talented."

Right. Cornelius, the Canine Ghost Whisperer. I

glance at Paco, who's struggling to lick a fleck of raspberry jam off his nose. More like the Scone Whisperer, if you ask me.

"Did the two of you, um...did you—"

"Did we participate in the séances?" Anthony finished. "Naturally. Miss Susan only hired staff who shared in her beliefs. It would have been too awkward otherwise."

"Do you have any idea how Abby Delgado might have gotten Cornelius? Is it possible that Susan might have left the dog to her?"

Anthony and Aurelia exchange a telling look. "Susan definitely did *not* leave Cornelius with that Delgado woman. Or with the other one either."

The other one?

"You mean, Phoebe Van Cleave?"

Aurelia makes a face. "Pushy woman, that one. Susan wasn't dead a day that she came sniffing around here trying to take Cornelius. She said that they *belonged* together. But Cornelius didn't like her."

"And he liked Abby?"

"He didn't dislike her, but we would never have given Cornelius away without Miss Deborah's consent. It wouldn't have been right."

"Then how did he end up with Abby? Deborah says that he ran away."

Anthony sets down his teacup. "Hardly. Corneluis would have never run away. He was dognapped."

I knew it! "For real?"

"We have security footage showing the culprit. But... Miss Deborah didn't want to involve the police."

So the whole story of Paco running away was just that. A story.

"Do you have proof that Abby Delgado stole Cornelius?"

"No," Anthony says firmly, "Not Miss Delgado. It was a man who took Cornelius."

"A man?" My heart speeds up. "Anthony, is there any way I can take a look at that footage?"

CHAPTER FOURTEEN

HOLY WOW. It's just as I suspected. Paco was dognapped by my favorite sociopath, Derrick Delgado.

After viewing the tape and promising Aurelia and Anthony that I'll keep in touch to let them know Cornelius's fate, I get in my car and head back to Whispering Bay.

PTSD, my butt. Wait till Will hears about this.

He sits on his living room couch with Paco on his lap listening to my story.

"I knew he was lying to the police, but now we have him on tape."

"You lied to the police, too. When you didn't tell Travis about how Abby was upset with Sebastian. But that doesn't mean you had anything to do with Abby's death."

I give Will the stink eye. "Whose side are you on?"

"I won't dignify that with an answer. So the brother

kidnapped the dog for Abby. All that proves is that they were in sync. He was probably doing her a favor."

"Then why lie about not knowing anything about the dog?"

"Maybe because what he did was illegal?"

"Which means that he's capable of doing *other* illegal activities. Like breaking and entering into the rec center."

"What's all this leading to?"

"We need to confront Derrick Delgado."

"*We?*"

"Yes, we. I can't just show up there on my own when he's already reported me to the police, can I?"

"The police?"

Oops.

"I forgot to tell you that part. When Derrick realized I didn't work for the law firm, he called the police. But only because he thought I was a scam artist, which goes to prove how unstable he is. I mean, really? *Me?* A scam artist?"

"I don't like this, Lucy."

"Does that mean you're out? Because I'm going to confront him with or without you."

"That's blackmail."

"So sue me."

He shakes his head as if he can't believe he's going to help me, then goes to the hall closet to pull out a jacket. "I'm driving."

"Awesome! Oh...and Will, just so you know, Derrick has a shotgun."

ME AND MY BIG MOUTH. If I hadn't told Will about Derrick's shotgun, he wouldn't have involved Travis.

"You were right to call me," Travis says to Will as we all pile into Will's car. He glares at me. "I thought you were going to update me on the dog?"

"I was. Eventually."

Travis is off duty, but the second he heard about my plans to confront Derrick he practically ran all the way to Will's house to join us. "For the record, I'm against this."

"Then go home," I say in a fake sweet voice.

"Believe me, I would if I didn't think you were going to hightail it over there no matter what Will or I say."

Will chuckles. "It's amazing how well you've come to know her in so little time."

"Sweet. I have two knights in shining armor." Despite my sarcasm, the truth is I'm glad that both Will and Travis are coming with me. I have no idea what Derrick Delgado is capable of, and I really don't want to find out on my own. Plus, you know, he does have that squirrel in his arsenal.

It's past eight p.m. by the time we get to Derrick's, and it's full-on dark. Since he lives on the edge of town on a dirt road, there aren't any street lights. Weeds cover the narrow path leading to the trailer. Luckily, Will keeps a couple of flashlights in the trunk of his car.

"Are you sure this is the address?" Will asks, aiming his light on the dented steel mailbox. The peel-on street numbers are faded from the sun making them difficult to read. I'm confident this is it, but I want to make sure, so I move the red side flag out of the way to get a better look at the numbers. It's so rusty and old that it falls off in my hands.

"This is the place, all right," I confirm.

"I can't believe you came out here all alone," Will says like a disapproving older brother. "Sebastian would have a cow if he knew you were running around confronting strange men with guns."

"How was I to know he'd pull a gun on me? Besides, all's well that ends well, right?"

Before Will can answer, the porch light snaps on.

"Who's out there?" asks a gruff male voice.

"Mr. Delgado, it's Officer Travis Fontaine from the Whispering Bay police department. I'd like to ask you a couple of questions."

The front door opens, and Derrick steps out. He's holding the infamous shotgun, but this time it's not aimed at anyone's head.

"Whoa." Travis points to the gun. "No need for that, sir."

Derrick's eyes go wide as he spots me. "That's her! That's the gal who tried to rob me."

"Rob you?" I sputter. "I admit, I *might* have misrepresented myself the other day, but believe me there is absolutely nothing you have that I'd want to rob you of."

He scowls at Will. "Who are you?"

"I'm a friend of Lucy's."

"So you're her accomplice."

Travis clears his throat. "About those questions, Mr. Delgado?"

"I ain't got nothing to hide, so ask away. But make it quick. I got a pot pie in the microwave."

"Miss McGuffin says she saw a surveillance tape that shows you jumping over a fence at Susan Van Dyke's house and stealing her dog. Do you know anything about that?"

Derrick's face registers shock for a second before he masks it with a sneer. "That's nuts. I don't know any Susan Van Dyke. And what the hell would I want with her dog?"

"Abby had Cornelius with her when she died. You dognapped him for her, didn't you?" I demand.

"Don't know what you're talking about, lady. Unless you're going to arrest me for something, then you bozos better get off my property."

Travis nods sternly. "Thank you for your cooperation, Mr. Delgado."

"*Cooperation?*" I turn to Travis. "That's *it*? You're aren't going to take him down to the police station? What kind of cop are you?"

A muscle on the side of Travis's jaw twitches. "Lucy, I told you before, leave this to the professionals."

Derrick grins like he knows he's got the upper hand. "Yeah, listen to the nice cop, *Lucy*."

The way he says my name gives me the heebie-jeebies.

Will takes me by the elbow. "Let's go," he says quietly. "We're not going to get anywhere by antagonizing him."

The last thing I want to do is leave. Not when I know

that Derrick is guilty of taking Paco and who knows what else. But I don't have any choice.

I start to follow Will down the steps, then I remember that I'm still holding onto the mail flag. I hand Derrick the rusty red flag. "By the way, this fell off your mailbox."

He looks at it a second, then tosses it into his yard. "I should sue you for the destruction of personal property, but I'm feelin' generous, so I'll just tell you to go on and get." He slams the door in our faces with a loud whack. A few seconds later the porch light goes out.

"Guess he wants to save on his electric bill," Will mutters.

"I really wish you'd let me ask the questions here," Travis says to me. "You forget this dognapping didn't happen in Whispering Bay. If Deborah Van Dyke doesn't want to press charges or get the Destin police involved, then there's not much I can do about it. I can't haul him down to the police station unless I have some evidence that he committed a crime in Whispering Bay. Got it?"

"So is breaking and entering into a public building considered a crime?"

"I'm not going to arrest Sebastian for that."

"Not yet anyway. What about Derrick? What if *he* broke into the building? What if he...what if he stole a key to the building and left it unlocked for some nefarious purpose?"

Travis looks at me like I've grown another head. "Where do you get this stuff?"

"I don't know, but if it did go down that way, then he

was definitely up to no good, and it's your responsibility as a police officer to get to the bottom of it."

"Okay, yeah. If that's the case, then, yeah, I'll arrest him. But good luck getting your proof. " He catches up to Will, who's already halfway to the car.

I hang back, slowly walking through the weedy yard, aiming the flashlight on the ground, until—*Bingo*!

I really can't believe our good luck.

I gingerly pick up the mailbox flag.

Will turns around and aims his light at me. "Lucy? What are you doing?" He winces when he sees the flag in my hand. "Unless your tetanus shot is up to date, I'd drop that."

"Yeah, I'd—" Travis stops when he sees the expression on my face. His frown is replaced with a grudging look of admiration.

"Oh," says Will, catching on as well.

"Yep," I say, grinning, "We just got Derrick Delgado's fingerprints."

CHAPTER FIFTEEN

"HA!" I shout gleefully from the backseat of the car. "Now all you have to do is match the fingerprints on that mail flag to the prints on the doorknob, and you'll have the proof you need. I can't wait to see the look on Derrick Delgado's face when you arrest him for breaking into the rec center."

Travis turns around in his seat to face me. "That's *if* the prints match. And even if they do that doesn't mean he entered the building illegally."

"Have you always had such a negative attitude? Good thing I was there when the technicians were dusting the doorknob. Don't forget my prints are going to be there too. Do you think I should be reprinted? So that the lab can tell whose prints belong to who?"

"The lab is perfectly capable of making that distinction," Travis says testily.

"Anyone want to stop for a burger and a shake?" Will asks. "I didn't have dinner so—"

"You're just mad because you didn't think to get Derrick's fingerprints," I say to Travis.

"Hardly. Like I said, even if his fingerprints are there, it doesn't necessarily mean anything."

"I know. I know. I should leave it to the *professionals*."

Travis makes a growling sound deep in his throat. "I admit, getting his fingerprints was pretty clever. Happy now?"

"Extremely."

Will catches my gaze in the rearview mirror. He looks confused.

"What?" I say to him. "Oh. The burger and shake. I'm good either way."

"Yeah," says Travis. "Stop if you want, or don't. It doesn't matter to me."

Will doesn't say anything, and he doesn't stop for food either. Instead, he drives back to his house in silence. Once there, Travis heads to the police station with the evidence I'm pretty sure is going to get Derrick in a lot of hot water. Or at least I hope so.

"Luce," Will says, stopping me as I'm about to get in my car, "What was all that about?"

"All what about?"

He pushes his glasses up his nose. "Between you and Travis. I know you don't like the guy, but that was a little extreme, don't you think?"

"Oh, *that*." I chuckle. "That was just some good-natured ribbing. Travis is...all right. A little stuffy, maybe, but we made our peace last night."

"Last night?"

"He came by my place after hours to talk about the case. He even ate one of my muffins. *And* he liked it. I was working on my newest batch of the mango coconut recipe. I think I'm really close to perfecting it."

Will nods thoughtfully, but I can tell something's bothering him. Only I have no idea what it might be, and he doesn't seem inclined to tell me, so we say our goodbyes, and I head to The Bistro.

Back home in my apartment, I settle in for my third night (and second in a row) with Paco, who insists on sleeping at the foot of my bed. I think I'm going to have to double my dose of Benadryl.

Even though I've basically taken enough medication to put me in a coma, I have trouble sleeping. I lay awake with Paco snuggled next to me, and I can't help but think about Susan Van Dyke. Anthony and Aurelia made her sound like she was a nice person. I really need to do right by this little dog of hers.

The next morning, I drag myself out of bed because once again I didn't fall asleep until after two. Paco, on the other hand, looks chirpy and refreshed. Currently, he's trotting back and forth between the apartment upstairs and the restaurant. He goes up to the patrons, happily accepting their pats on his head, and never begs or makes a pest of himself.

It's as if he's on his best behavior, showing me what a great addition he'd make to The Bistro. Unfortunately, his nice dog routine isn't going to work with me because I can't live on Benadryl forever.

Just as I think that I need to call Lanie to update her on the dog situation, she and Dharma walk through the door. Paco immediately runs up to be petted.

"Hey, little guy!" Lanie scoops him up and kisses him on the nose. "Isn't he adorable?" she asks Dharma.

Dharma gazes at Paco warily.

"I thought you were bringing him back to Susan Van Dyke's family," says Lanie.

I fill them in on what happened yesterday, including the fact that Paco was dognapped by Derrick Delgado.

"Wow. That's crazy. So he needs a permanent home, huh?"

"Babe," Dharma says firmly like she already knows where this is headed, "we already have four dogs. You promised. Not one more."

"But—" The look on Dharma's face stops Lanie mid-sentence. "Dharma is right. It wouldn't be fair to Paco if we took him. Between our jobs, we barely have time for the four we have." She reluctantly places Paco down on the floor.

"I understand." *Rats.* I was really hoping that Lanie would take him. "Will you be on the lookout for a good family? Someone who'll really appreciate him? I don't mind keeping him until you find the right person."

"Sure thing, Lucy."

I hate taking medication, but it's just temporary until Paco finds his forever home. Maybe Dr. Nate can prescribe something that makes me less drowsy than the Benadryl. I make a mental note to call his office to set up an appointment.

I take their orders and pour them coffee, when out of the blue, Paco starts barking like he's possessed. I've never seen him like this before. I'm about to apologize to the next customer in line when I see that it's Phoebe Van Cleave and her ghost society pals.

Phoebe takes one look at the dog and goes pale.

Ha! I should tell her that I'm on to her. How I know all about how she wanted Cornelius, and that's she not fooling anybody. Especially not me.

"It's Cornelius!" Victor crouches down to Paco's eye level. "What are you doing here?"

Paco keeps barking.

"This is the dog that Abby had with her when she passed," I say, trying to gauge everyone's reactions.

No one, not even Gloria seems surprised by this, which is pretty telling.

"Paco," I say, "stop it. You're disturbing the customers."

"Paco?" says Victor.

"I'm calling him that, since it's the name Abby gave him."

Paco barks one more time for good measure, then lets out a final growl and runs up the stairs back to the apartment. Not that I blame him. If I were him, I'd want to get as far away from Phoebe as I could too. "Sorry, I don't think he likes you."

Phoebe sniffs. "I don't understand. He's never reacted like this to me before."

Gloria nods in agreement. "Cornelius, er, that is, Paco and I have done several séances together at Susan's home, and he's always been extremely charming. What do you think got into him?"

"Considering that his owner died, then a few days later he was dognapped, and then he was with poor Abby when she passed, I'd say he might have some trauma going on."

"*Dognapped!*" Gloria says. "Who on earth would do that?"

The hairs on my neck tingle. Gloria isn't as shocked by this information as she wants me to think she is.

"Derrick Delgado. He denies it, but there's a surveillance tape that proves otherwise."

If I thought Phoebe was pale before, then it's nothing compared to now. It's like all the blood has drained from her face. "This is so disturbing," she murmurs.

Victor tsks. "I'll say." He studies me closely. "How have you been, Lucy?"

I mentally sigh because I know what's coming next. "I haven't gotten any messages from Abby if that's what you want to know."

The three of them exchange a look.

"If you'd agree to participate in a séance," says Gloria, "Maybe we could find out why Abby's brother dognapped Paco."

I'm about to ixnay the séance idea when I snap my mouth shut. It occurs to me that I've been looking at this all wrong. Phoebe knows a lot more about this dognapping than she's let on. Gloria and probably Victor do, too. But Phoebe is the only one of them with a motive to get rid of Abby. I'd bet my last mixing bowl that Phoebe is at least partially responsible for fast tracking Abby along to the pearly gates.

Not in a million years do I think a séance trying to communicate with Abby's spirit is going to work, but Phoebe believes in it, and that's what matters. Maybe it will be the catalyst for her to confess everything she knows.

"Now that you mention it, maybe Abby *has* been trying to communicate with me."

"I knew it!" says Gloria.

"Really?" Victor gazes behind me like there's something there. "Do you think she's here now?"

"Sure. At least I think so. I really can't tell because, you know, I'm not trained to look for any of the signs."

"That's it. We absolutely need to do a séance," Gloria persists. "Abby is practically calling to us from the grave."

Victor nods enthusiastically. "I agree."

"Oh, I don't think a séance is necessary," says Phoebe.

Gloria and Victor turn and stare at her. There's only one reason Phoebe wouldn't want to do a séance. And that's because she's afraid of what we'll find out. Which means I want to do this more than ever.

Sarah comes up to the counter to refill the coffee pot. "Did someone just say séance?" She looks like she's trying not to laugh.

"Lucy has agreed to help us talk to Abby," Gloria says.

Sarah's jaw goes slack before she pulls her expression together. "Really?"

"I just want to help," I say trying to sound innocent.

"And of course, Paco will need to be there," says Victor.

"I don't think that's a good idea," Phoebe says. "Didn't you just say that the dog has been through a trauma? To expect him to participate in a séance so soon after all he's been through... no. It's inhumane. Also, Lucy, dear, I couldn't help but overhear part of your conversation with Lanie Miller. It seems like you're looking for a home for the little angel? As I said before, I'll be happy to take him. As a matter of fact, I practically consider it my civic duty."

Gloria puts her arm around Phoebe's shoulder. "I'm sorry to be so blunt, but do you think that's a good idea considering that the dog doesn't like you?"

"Gloria's right," says Victor. "He seems to be fairly aggressive toward you."

Phoebe looks like she's going to cry. "I don't understand why he suddenly doesn't like me."

"Thanks for offering, but Paco has already been adopted," I blurt.

"He has?" Sarah asks.

Oh boy. How am I going to get out of this one?

"Yep. My brother wants him. Yes, that's right, my brother, the priest, wants Paco."

It's been my experience that whenever you add "the priest" in any sort of communication, people back down. It seems to work here too because no one questions me anymore.

"That was fast," Phoebe mutters.

Gloria lowers her voice. "So, about the séance...."

CHAPTER SIXTEEN

GLORIA LAYS DOWN ALL the conditions for the "ideal" séance environment. They're a bit wacky, but what do I know about talking to the dead? All I know is that to pull this off, I'm going to need help from my best friend.

It kills me to have to wait till The Bistro closes for the day, but I've already left work early twice this week, and it wouldn't be fair to Sarah if I take off again. Once all the customers are gone and the kitchen is clean, I put Paco in my car and head over to Will's.

He's just getting home from the library at the same time I pull into his driveway. He looks exhausted, which doesn't make sense since he took some vacation days this week.

"Big run on Hemingway today?" I ask.

He grins at my joke. "Been cataloguing a new shipment." He unlocks his front door to let us all in. "Hey, little guy," he says, rubbing the top of Paco's head affectionately.

"You wouldn't happen to be in the market for a dog, would you?"

Why didn't I think of this before?

It makes so much sense. Will isn't allergic. He's kind to animals. Paco already likes him. And he's already offered to take him once, even though it was just for the night. If Will adopts Paco, then I can see Paco all the time. It's a total win-win scenario.

"Lanie Miller wasn't interested?"

"She was. Dharma wasn't. So, how about it?"

"I don't know, Luce. He seems like a great dog, but I'm at work all day. I'm too busy to give him the kind of attention he'll need."

"But he doesn't need much," I protest. "And I'd help."

"What about Sebastian?"

"I already thought about him. He's my last resort, but he's busier than all of us combined."

"I wish I could, but—stop it."

"Stop what?"

"Doing that thing with your eyes."

"What am I doing with my eyes?"

"Making them all sad looking. It's like you have deer eyes."

I giggle. No one has ever told me I have deer eyes before. "Okay, I'll try to look mean."

He sighs. "Look, if you can't find anyone else to take the dog, then I'll do it."

"Really?"

"Sure, why not?"

"Thanks! Hey, by the way, what you do know about an author named J.W. Quicksilver? Apparently, he writes these intense thrillers."

"Never heard of him."

"Really? I thought you were supposed to be a librarian. Anyway, Betty Jean's book club is reading his latest. She promised me lots of big action and hot sex."

He looks at me over the top of his glasses. "You're joining Betty Jean's book club?"

"It's a big honor," I tease. "She says she'll push me to the top of the waiting list if I bring muffins."

Before Will can respond, my cell phone pings. "Yes! It's Travis. I've been waiting all day for this call." Will opens his mouth to say something, but I put a hand up in the air to stop him. "Did the prints match?"

Travis makes a grumpy sound.

"I'll take that as a yes?"

"Don't get all bigheaded, but you were right. Derrick Delgado's fingerprints are on the doorknob from the rec center. We already had his prints on file. He was arrested ten years ago for assaulting a guy during a bar fight."

No big surprise there. "You're going to arrest him, right?"

"No. I'm going to bring him in and question him. But you're getting your hopes up for nothing. We don't have any evidence of wrongdoing. For all we know he's going to tell us that he was at the rec center during the opening celebration and that's when he touched the doorknob."

"Only you know it wouldn't be true."

"And how would I know that exactly?"

If only I could be there when Derrick is being questioned, I'd be able to tell Travis if he's lying or not. Except, no, that wouldn't work because it would mean telling Travis about my gift. His dad, I trust. But Travis...it isn't that I don't trust him. And it's not even that I think he won't believe me. But he would definitely think I was strange, and for some unknown reason, I don't want that.

"Is there any way I can be there when you question him?"

"Absolutely not."

"You're no fun."

"Sure I am. You just haven't been around me long enough." The way Travis says this, it sounds almost...flirty. He clears his throat. "So you're not going to like this, but I wanted you to hear it from me first. We're also going to bring your brother in for questioning."

"You're kidding."

"No, Lucy, I'm not. He knows something, and he refuses to cooperate. I have no choice. If he were anyone else, this would have happened three days ago."

Logically, I know that Travis is right. But I still hate that my brother is being dragged into this. I have to find out what went on in that rec center the night Abby died. Which means this séance has to happen.

"Thanks for the heads up," I say grudgingly. When I get off the phone, Will is staring at me as if I've done something wrong. "What?"

"Nothing." But he sounds moody, and that isn't like him.

"So, the reason I came over here is because I need a favor. And you aren't going to like it."

Will opens his refrigerator and takes out two beers. He hands me one. "Why aren't I going to like it?"

I wait till he's taken a sip of the beer and looks relaxed before I say, "Because it's sort of illegal. But totally for a good reason. I need to get a small, *very* small group, into the rec center at midnight so we can have a séance. And since the center is normally closed that means we'll basically have to break in."

Beer comes sputtering out of Will's mouth and spills onto the leather sofa. Paco runs to lick it up. "You want me to help you break into the rec center?" he asks incredulously. "Isn't this the same thing you want Derrick Delgado locked up for?"

"That's different. I'm this close," I say, putting my thumb and index finger up so that they're practically touching, "to finding out what really happened the night Abby died. And I do *not* have PTSD I just need this séance to help put the pieces of the puzzle together."

"Are you listening to yourself? When did you start believing in this stuff?"

"I don't believe the séance is going to work, silly. But Phoebe does. That's the important part. These people think that Abby is linked to me. So all I have to do is fake it, and once Phoebe thinks she's talking to Abby, I'll get her to confess everything she knows."

Will closes his eyes for a moment like he's trying to absorb all this. "Let's say I thought this was a good idea, which I don't. Why does the séance have to be in the rec center? Why can't it be in someone's spooky old house? Or better yet, in a graveyard?"

"Right? The rec center is Gloria's stipulation. She says we need to do the séance in the rec center because that's where Abby died, and we need to do it as close to the time of her death as possible. Which means we need to do it around one in the morning. Oh, and Paco needs to be there too because you know, they think he sees dead people, and that could really come in handy."

"And you don't think this all sounds crazy?"

"Maybe. A little." He glares at me. "Okay, maybe more than a little. All I know is that my gut is telling me Phoebe had something to do with Abby's death. And...now the cops want to bring Sebastian in for questioning. And you know him. He'll never tell them anything that he thinks might be breaking some sort of sacred confidence. Even if the cops go easy on him, there will always be a cloud of suspicion hanging over his head unless we can figure out what he and Abby were doing in the rec center."

Will sighs wearily. "What do you need from me?"

"You're the head librarian, which makes you an important public employee, right? Isn't there some kind of master key to all the city-owned buildings?"

"No."

"Okay, well, Gus had a set of keys to the building during the celebration. Who usually has those?"

"I would imagine that the rec center director has those. And probably some of the class instructors."

"Like Viola?"

"Yeah, she might have a set of keys. If she ever opens or locks up the building. But..." Will shakes his head in disbelief. "I can't believe I'm about to say this. I think I know who might have a set of keys."

"Really? Who?"

"Brittany. She teaches the evening Pilates class. She said something about having to lock up after class the other day."

Fate must be laughing in my face right now because the last person I want to be indebted to is Brittany Kelly. "Do you think she'll help?"

"I don't know, Lucy. She could get in a lot of trouble. We all could."

"Not if we don't get caught."

He snorts.

"Please. Will you ask her?" I decide to play my ace again. "For Sebastian?"

"Let me think about it."

"Thanks, Will!"

"I said I'd think about it. I was going to call her later this evening to solidify our plans for Friday night. I'll throw some feelers out and see if I can gauge her reaction. If she shuts it down even a little, which she probably will, then I'm not going to pursue it. Understand?"

Since this is the best I can hope for, I nod eagerly. "Sure, thanks. Speaking of Brittany, where are you taking her on the big date?"

"I was thinking of that steak place in Seaside. Then maybe a walk along the beach afterward. What do you think? Too lame?"

There's no such thing as too lame for Brittany.

"Sounds perfect."

Neither of us say anything for a few beats.

My cell phone rings. It's too soon for it be Travis again, so I'm about to decline the call when I notice the area code. "Oh my God. It's the Cooking Channel!" I'm too excited and shocked to move.

Will's eyes light up. "Lucy, you're on the show."

"What if they're calling to turn me down?"

"They'd do that in an email. Go on," he urges, "answer the phone."

I take a deep breath and press the accept button. "Hello," I croak.

"Is this Lucy McGuffin?" asks a female voice.

"Yes, that's me."

"This is Tamara Hayes from The Cooking Channel. How are you today?" She sounds upbeat, which is a positive sign. Right?

"I'm good. I think."

She chuckles, but it sounds more practiced than sincere. "I've had a chance to go over your application, and I've seen your audition tape. You're fabulous, by the way! A complete natural!"

"I am?"

"The camera loves you, Lucy, and the camera doesn't love everyone. I'm *thrilled* to tell you that we're moving you on to the next phase of the auditions."

"There's another phase?"

"Oh yes. We'll be sending a camera crew to your kitchen. To get a feel for the locale, that kind of thing. You'll receive an email with an attachment that explains every-thing." I can hear her shuffling some papers around. "Let's see...your café is called The Bistro by the Beach, and you own it along with a Sarah Powers?"

"That's right."

"Fabulous. Of course, we'll need Sarah to agree to the filming, and she'll need to sign all the waivers."

"Sure! She's just as excited about this as I am."

"Marvelous. We'll be in touch soon. Ciao!"

I click the disconnect button in a daze.

"Are you on the show?" Will asks eagerly.

"Not yet. There's one more phase to the auditions."

"Lucy, that's awesome."

"It is, isn't?"

And then because it feels natural, I reach out and hug him and he gives me a quick sisterly hug back. I wish he didn't feel so solid or smell so good. My life would be a whole lot easier if Will and I were on the same page here.

"Do they go to all the contestants' hometowns before they decide to put them on the show?" he asks.

"I don't know. Maybe this is part of the intro package. You know, when they're telling the audience about the contestants. Only you'd think they'd only film those with the people they've already picked."

"Seems to me that you're a shoo-in."

"Thanks. But you have to say that because you're my best friend, which reminds me, if I win *Muffin Wars*, I'll be able to pay you back the money you loaned me for the down payment on The Bistro."

"No worries. Pay me back whenever you can."

"No worries? Ten grand had to have put a big dent in your savings."

"It's a great investment," he says, sounding uncomfortable the way he always does whenever I mention the loan. "Have you thought about how you're going to fake like you're talking to Abby Delgado's spirit?"

"That's the easy part. I just have to watch *Ghost* again and get my Whoopi on."

"That'll make, what? The hundredth time you've seen it?"

Will knows that *Ghost* is one of my favorite movies. The pottery wheel scene between Patrick Swayze and Demi Moore always makes my heart do flip flops. I've made him watch it at least three times. He pretends that he hates it, but deep down, I know he gets a big kick out of the whole who's-good-and-who's-bad theme.

"So I'll make it a hundred and one. Your job is to convince Brittany to let us use her key to get into the building."

"That's if she even has a key."

"I have every confidence in your abilities to persuade her."

He shakes his head. "Sometimes being your best friend is a lot of work, Lucy."

"But you wouldn't want it any other way. Right?"

He hesitates just a fraction of a second too long before he answers. "Right."

CHAPTER SEVENTEEN

AFTER I LEAVE Will's house, I take Paco to the park, where he behaves like a perfect little gentleman. Every five minutes I check my phone to see if either Will or Travis has called to update me on their respective assignments.

When a good hour goes by, and I don't hear from either of them, I decide to take matters into my own hands. I'm about to dial Travis when my cell rings.

"Hello?"

"Lucy? It's Aurelia Finch, Susan Van Dyke's cook."

"Oh! Hi, Aurelia."

"Anthony and I were wondering how Cornelius was faring. Have you found a permanent home for him yet?"

"I'm pretty confident I can talk my best friend Will into taking him. He'd be terrific with the dog."

"The sweet little thing has been through so much. I feel better knowing that you're looking out for his welfare."

Now that I have Aurelia on the phone, I realize she's the perfect person to give me some intel. "When Susan was alive, you said that she used to host séances in her home? And that Cornelius assisted?"

"Oh, yes. She couldn't have done them without him. He's a very gifted medium."

"Good to know because he's going to be participating in another séance soon. Maybe even as soon as tomorrow night. Is there anything I should know about how to prep him? Any special foods or anything?"

"No special prep is needed, but I should warn you. Talking to the dead isn't a trifling thing. This has to be done correctly, or who knows what might happen. If the environment isn't carefully monitored, it can turn dangerous for Cornelius."

Dangerous? It occurs to me that I'm clueless here. "Exactly how does Cornelius whisper to the dead?"

"Cornelius makes contact with the spirit we're calling to. Then the human medium picks up on Cornelius's vibrations and communicates those vibrations back to the other members of the séance. If the human medium isn't talented enough to sense what Cornelius is feeling, then all those thoughts can be trapped inside him and create an unhealthy chi."

Just as I thought. It's all a big bunch of hooey. "Got it."

Aurelia tsks. "I'd already pegged you as a non-believer, but I didn't know you were also a cynic."

Oops. "Sorry, I didn't mean to sound skeptical."

"It's all right. Anthony and I are used to it. Who's in charge of this séance?"

"The Sunshine Ghost Society, so Madame Gloria will be the, um, human medium."

"I see."

It's not hard to figure out what Aurelia thinks of that. "I know you're not crazy about Phoebe Van Cleave, but the rest of the group isn't so bad."

"Whose spirit will they be talking to?"

"Hopefully, Abby Delgado's."

"You know, Lucy, Anthony and I were an integral part of the séances that Susan used to host. Since this is the first séance that Cornelius will be doing without Susan, perhaps we should be there too. For moral support."

"Sure. Why not? Except.... I have to tell you, we're using a building without permission."

"Oh dear."

I tell her about the conditions Gloria put down for the séance.

"She's correct. The spirit does tend to linger in places where he or she was last alive."

"So I've been told. I'm really hoping that we can get to the bottom of why Abby's brother stole Cornelius." *Among other things.*

"I take it the brother didn't confess?"

"Hardly. And since Deborah doesn't want to press charges, there's nothing the Whispering Bay police can do about it."

"Nothing?"

"Well, I did manage to get the brother's fingerprints without him knowing it." I can't help but brag. "They matched a set of prints on the doorknob to the rec center where his sister was found. Travis Fontaine, that's the police officer in charge of Abby's case, is bringing him in for questioning. They might not be able to get him for dognapping, but there's a possibility they could charge him for trespassing, which is better than nothing."

"How clever you are," she muses.

"Thanks, not that it will do much good. Even though I think he had something to do with his sister's death, he has an alibi."

"The police checked it out?"

"Yep. Derrick was at home in Mexico Beach playing cards till two in the morning. It's an hour away, so even if he left right at two, he couldn't have gotten to Whispering Bay till three a.m. earliest, which puts it a little too far off from the time Abby died."

"Mexico Beach? Anthony and I have been there. It's an adorable little town."

"Yeah, well, he lives in the not so adorable part. Almost in the boonies, really."

"To the east?" she asks.

I still as Aurelia's words sink in.

Holy wow. Why didn't I think of this before?

Mexico Beach sits directly on the line between the eastern and central time zones. I'm pretty sure that Derrick's house lies in what the north Florida natives refer to as "fast time" or Eastern Standard Time. Whispering

Bay, on the other hand, sits in "slow time" or Central Standard Time. Which means that two in the morning at Derrick's place was one in the morning in Whispering Bay, giving him plenty of time to get to the rec center during the time period that the coroner placed her death.

I need to get this information to Travis ASAP.

THE WHISPERING BAY POLICE DEPARTMENT is located on the gulf right next to the city municipal building. Since there isn't a sign on the door that explicitly says no dogs allowed, I bring Paco inside. "Better to ask forgiveness than permission." Paco wags his tail like he agrees.

Cindy, the receptionist, looks up from her computer screen. She and Rusty have been dating for about a year now. She's another good customer of mine, although she hasn't been to The Bistro in over a week, which can only mean that she's dieting again. Her favorite muffin is cranberry raisin. Maybe I can come up with a low-fat version.

"Hey, Cindy. Is there any way I can see Travis Fontaine? It's kind of an emergency."

She shakes her head. "You too, Lucy?"

"What do you mean?"

"Just that every single woman under the age of thirty-five has come by in the last week on some pretext or another to see Travis."

A part of me finds this amusing. Another part finds it... irritating. "I guess there's no accounting for taste."

Paco whimpers, drawing attention to himself.

"Oh! I didn't see your dog." Cindy leans over her desk and pats him on the head. "When did you get him? What's his name?"

"I'm watching him temporarily. His name is Paco."

"Hey little guy," Cindy croons.

He makes a big show of wagging his tail and looking utterly adorable like he's trying to win her over, only I'm pretty sure he's already done that.

"I could just die, you're so cute!" Cindy reaches into the top drawer of her desk and pulls out a granola bar. "Is it okay if I give him a piece?"

Paco barks as if to say *yes, please!*

"Sure, why not?"

She ends up giving him the entire granola bar, and even though I fed him just a couple of hours ago, he gobbles it down like he's starving,

"So, Cindy, Travis told me that he was bringing Derrick Delgado in for questioning. Do you know how that went? Is it still going on?"

And more importantly, is Derrick in handcuffs yet?

"Well, I'm not supposed to say, since it's official police business and all."

Paco nudges me with his nose like he's urging me to try another tactic. If I didn't know better, I'd think that he understood what we were saying. "Did you know that I was the one who found Abby Delgado?"

"Rusty told me. Bless your heart. That must have been awful! Did you have to do CPR?"

"No, but it was still traumatic," I say playing it up.

"I know what you mean. Rusty and I were at The Harbor House a couple of weeks ago to celebrate our one-year anniversary, and the man in the table next to us started to choke. It was horrible. His face turned red as a tomato. Rusty was a real hero," she adds proudly.

"Did he have to do the Heimlich maneuver?"

"He was the one who dialed 911."

"And they saved the guy?"

"Actually...no. By the time the paramedics got there, one of the waiters had done the Heimlich." She shrugs like that part of the story is inconsequential.

I lean in closer to her desk. "Cindy, did you know that Officer Fontaine is planning to bring my brother in for questioning?"

She squirms in her chair. "Rusty mentioned something about that."

"How did Officer Fontaine get put in charge of this case? I mean, doesn't Rusty have seniority over him?"

"Yes, but Zeke thinks that Travis practically walks on water. Rusty has been with the department for twenty years. Then this hot shot swoops in and just because he's from Dallas everyone thinks he knows so much more."

"That's so unfair."

"Tell me about it."

I sigh dramatically. "I bet if Rusty were in charge, we'd already know what happened to Abby."

Even though there's no one else in the room, she lowers

her voice. "I guess it won't hurt to tell you that Derrick Delgado is in the interrogation room as we speak."

My heart speeds up. "Really?"

She nods. "Rusty and Travis are in there with him now. You should have seen him strut in here like he owned the place! I've worked here a long time, and I can always tell when someone's guilty. It's the eyes. His are shifty as hell."

"Oh, believe me, I've had the displeasure of speaking to the man twice, and I totally agree." *If I could just get into that interrogation room somehow...* "Cindy, Officer Fontaine mentioned that there was surveillance footage that showed both Abby and my brother Sebastian entering the rec center the night she died."

"Oh, yeah, I've seen it."

"You have?" I can barely contain my excitement. "Do you think it would be okay if I took a look at it? I mean, maybe I can pick up something that *Officer* Fontaine didn't." I made sure to add a snarky tone to my voice whenever I say Travis's name.

"Golly, Lucy, I wish I could show it to you, but I don't think Zeke would like that."

"I understand. It's just...Officer Fontaine hinted that he was going to use the tape to press charges against Sebastian. For trespassing into the rec center."

Okay, so this isn't *exactly* true, but it works because Cindy looks mortified. "*Arrest* Father McGuffin? I can't believe it! He's going too far now."

"I agree. But what can we do?"

She thinks this over. "I don't see how it would hurt for you to take a look at the footage."

"Really? You're a complete doll!"

Cindy pulls an empty chair up to her desk. I place Paco on my lap, and we both look on as she taps on her computer screen. "It should come up any minute."

A series of black and white images appear. "See," she says, pointing to the top of the screen, "here's the date and time." The date reads November 3 and the time is set at 11:55 pm. We watch for the next five minutes as nothing happens. Then there's a shot of Abby walking along the side of the building. She stops at the door, jiggles the lock and walks in.

"So the door was already open," I say to myself.

Cindy fast-forwards to twelve thirty, when Sebastian shows up. He stands in front of the door, and even though the camera angle doesn't show his face clearly, I can tell by his body language that he's hesitant to walk inside. But after a few seconds, he opens the door and enters the building.

Nothing else happens for the next few minutes or so. At precisely twelve thirty-five, Sebastian walks out the building through the same door.

"That's all there is to see," Cindy says.

Something here isn't right. Only I'm not sure what it is.

"What about earlier? How far back has anyone looked?"

"I just told you. That's all there is."

I still. "You mean, that's *all* the security footage that's available? From any of the doors?"

Cindy nods. "The system was getting revamped, and

the cameras weren't fully operational until just a few days ago."

I remember now that during the rec center celebration Gus said something along those lines.

"So there could be lots of people who came and went at some other time or through other doors, but they weren't caught on camera?"

"Sure. I mean, yeah, who knows?"

Except the footage doesn't show anyone else entering or leaving the building. Which means that Sebastian is the last person who saw Abby alive.

Ha! No wonder I thought Travis was lying to me. He purposely misled me about the security footage because he wanted me to get Sebastian to tell him what he and Abby were doing in the building. That sneaky little...

I begrudgingly have to admire his tactics.

"Can I see the footage one more time?"

We rewatch the film. This time I'm on super alert for any little thing. Only nothing stands out.

Paco nudges me with his nose.

"Not now, sweetie."

He nudges harder.

"Paco, what do you—" I glance down at him. He looks back at me with those sweet brown eyes, and I swear he's trying to tell me something. If I've learned anything over the past week, it's that I should listen to this little dog. "Do you mind if we watch it again?"

Cindy shrugs. "Why not?" She sets the recording back. Five minutes later, we watch once more as Abby goes through the motion of trying the lock and walking through the door.

"Holy wow," I mutter. "Can you freeze that?"

"What? Do you see something?" Cindy pushes the pause button.

I turn to look at her. "When I found Abby, Paco was with her."

"Poor tyke. It must have been traumatic for him."

"Yeah, but don't you see? According to the footage, Abby goes into the rec center, but she's alone. The dog wasn't with her. Which means Paco must have *already* been in the rec center when she got there."

"Are you sure about that?"

"Positive. Sebastian specifically told me when he saw Abby she had the dog with her."

"So someone else brought the dog into the rec center?"

"Yep. And I'd bet a dozen of my best apple walnut cream cheese muffins that it's the same person who unlocked the door. If we can find out who had the key, then we'll know...well, we'll know something important, that's for sure."

"Golly." She glances nervously off to the side. "And you think maybe it was the brother?"

"He has a pretty good motive for wanting to get rid of Abby. She left him everything. And he certainly likes to wave a gun around. Plus, Officer Fontaine told me Derrick's been arrested before. For assault."

Cindy shudders. "I get so worried when Rusty has to deal with these criminal types."

Since Rusty is a cop, I'm not sure what to say here.

"Rusty and Travis have been interrogating Derrick for a while now, huh?"

She nods. "At least thirty minutes."

"I sure would love to know what's going on in there."

Cindy doesn't say anything.

"You know, on T.V. they always show those interrogations taking place in one room while another cop is in the next room looking through one of those two-way mirrors and listening in through a speaker."

"Oh yeah, isn't that cool?"

"The Whispering Bay police department wouldn't happen to have one of those rooms, would they?"

"Nah. We're not big enough for anything that fancy."

"Oh." I can't hide my disappointment.

"But we have an intercom system."

"Really?"

"Sure. That way if someone in the room needs something they just have to call out for it. And vice versa. If I need to speak to the cop in the room, then I just call in."

"So, you could also use the intercom to listen in?"

Cindy's cheeks go red. "Technically, I suppose I could do that."

Technically, my butt. Cindy has listened in before. And not just once or twice either.

"Thirty minutes seems like a long time to be interrogating someone about a simple trespassing case, doesn't it?" I let that sink in. "You know, I would never tell anyone if you accidentally hit the intercom button."

She wets her bottom lip. "If we make any noise, then they'll know we're listening."

"I promise, I'll be quiet as a mouse."

She smiles coyly. "Okay." She hits a button next to her phone.

Derrick's voice is the first one we hear. "So I took the dog. Sue me."

Well, this at least is the truth.

At the sound of Derrick's voice, Paco's body goes tense. Using my eyes, I plead with him to stay silent. Luckily, he seems to understand.

"The dog was being abused," Derrick continues. "Left out in the yard with no food or water. The way I see it, I was doing the mutt a favor. You said no one was pressin' charges so draggin' me down here today is total crap."

"What about your fingerprints on the doorknob at the rec center?" Travis asks.

"Didn't know it was a crime to touch a door."

"It isn't. But it is a crime to trespass into a city building after hours."

"Look. I told you already. I took the dog because Abby asked me to. She gave me a couple of hundred bucks for my trouble, which I appreciated, you know? You try living on social security. But that was it. End of story. I probably touched the doorknob during that big...what was it? Celebration? Yeah, that's when it must have happened."

"You were at the opening day celebration?" Rusty asks.

"Sure. I promised Abby I'd meet her, but she never showed so I went home."

This is such a big lie that I can hardly catch a breath.

"Okay," says Travis.

"So I can go home now?"

"Yeah."

The sound of chairs scraping against the floor makes Cindy snap off the intercom button. "I think they're coming out now," she whispers.

A minute later, Derrick Delgado emerges from the hallway, followed by Rusty and Travis. Paco goes wild barking. I scoop him up in my arms.

The look on Derrick's face when he spots me is priceless. Like I'm some pesky wad of gum he's tossed out the window that's come back to hit him in the face. "What are *you* doing here?"

"This is a public building. I have every right to be here."

Paco bares his teeth at Derrick.

"Keep that mongrel away from me. Or I'll have animal control put him down."

This is entirely the *wrong* thing to say to me.

"Funny how he seems not to like you. Oh, wait. I guess that since you *dognapped* him, he's a little sensitive around you. Deborah Van Dyke might not have wanted to press charges before, but when I tell her that you've also been arrested for assault, she just might change her mind. She might consider it her civic duty to put you away."

"Can't you make her shut up?" Derrick says to Travis.

"Lucy," Travis warns. "Leave it alone."

"How many times are you going to let this guy get away with who knows what?" I ask. "He wasn't at the rec center celebration, that's for sure. Oh, and ask him about his alibi! He might have been playing cards till two in the morning, but it was two in the morning *eastern* time. Which means he had plenty of time to drive over here, get inside the building, and—"

"And what?" Derrick sneers. He turns to Travis. "Are you gonna let her talk to me like this? I'm a grieving brother, and this crazy lady is harassing me."

"He's right, Lucy. You need to cut it out."

"But he was lying about how his fingerprints got on the doorknob! He was never at the rec center celebration. And if he's lying about that, then he could be lying about everything else too."

Travis frowns. "How do you know he told us he was at the rec center celebration?"

Oops. I can't very well tell Travis how I know that without getting Cindy into trouble.

"It was a lucky guess."

Everyone is looking at me like I've gone bananas. Except Cindy who won't meet my gaze.

Derrick jabs a finger at me. "I want her arrested and that damn dog put down! He's a menace. Look at him! She's probably trained him to attack me!"

I'm about to open my mouth when Travis puts a hand up in the air, stopping me.

"Mr. Delgado," he says, "Thank you for coming down here today to answer our questions. You're free to go home."

As he's leaving out the door, he brushes past me on purpose and leers. "I better not catch you trying to break into my place again. You or that damn little dog you like so much."

How I manage to hold my tongue is beyond me, but I do.

A full minute goes by before anyone says anything.

"Wow," says Rusty. "That sure was intense."

Travis motions me toward the back of the hallway. "Can I have a word with you? In private?" The way he says it doesn't sound like a request. More like an order.

Cindy and Rusty immediately go to work appearing busy. She starts typing on her computer and Rusty rifles through a stack of papers on his desk, but I can tell they're both dying to know whatever it is Travis is going to say to me.

Unfortunately, I have a pretty good idea already.

Paco, who's calmed down considerably since Derrick left, nudges to be let down. We follow Travis to the alcove.

"Before you say anything, I know I was a little out of line—"

"A *little*? How about a lot?"

"I can't believe you're going to let Derrick get away with...everything he's done."

"What's he done? Other than taking the dog? Which, I might add, we've already established we can't do anything about."

"That's just it, we don't know, because there's no video evidence, is there?"

He looks taken aback. "What do you mean?"

"You didn't lie when you said that the footage only

showed Abby and Sebastian going into the rec center because that's the only footage that exists. The truth is, you have *no* idea who went into that building the night Abby died because most of the cameras weren't operational until the day after the rec center officially opened."

"It doesn't matter anyway, because this case is closed. The autopsy report just came in a few minutes ago. Abby died of a heart attack with no evidence of any foul play, and no trespassing charges are going to be filed. Against *anyone*. I just left your brother a message telling him not to bother coming down for questioning."

"A heart attack?"

Travis nods wearily.

"But what about the fall? Didn't she hit her head?"

"The coroner can't tell which came first, the heart attack or the fall. There's a pretty good chance that the fall was caused by her heart attack."

"And that's *it*?"

"Yeah, that's it." He frowns. "I thought you'd be happy that Sebastian is off the hook."

"Of course I'm happy. But...don't you still want to know what Abby was doing in the rec center in the first place?"

"No, I don't. Right now there are two cops out with the flu, and the chief has his hands full at home, so I'd appreciate it if you stop trying to make more work for the department. In the future, I suggest you stick to doing what you do best. Stay away from my crime scenes, and I'll stay out of your kitchen."

"So, you admit it was a crime scene."

He rakes a hand through his hair. "That was a figure of speech. I mean it, Lucy, the next time you interfere with an official police investigation I'm not going to be so easygoing about the whole thing. Now if you don't mind? I have work to do." He stomps off down the hall, leaving Paco and me to stare after him.

CHAPTER EIGHTEEN

SO MUCH FOR getting the new information to Travis ASAP. And to think, I was just beginning to like him. Well, not like *like* him, but he was almost tolerable.

It's as if he doesn't want to listen to reason. Or maybe, I'm the one who doesn't want to listen. Maybe Abby's death was just like Travis said—completely natural with no sign of foul play.

Only my gut tells me that something sinister happened in that rec center. I'll never rest until I know what Abby and my brother were doing there in the middle of the night, and there's only one person who can tell me that. Since it's Wednesday afternoon, I know exactly where to find him. St. Perpetua's Catholic Church holds weekly reconciliations *aka* confessions every Wednesday from four to six p.m. There's no way Sebastian can avoid me there.

I hastily drop Paco off at The Bistro then head over to see my brother. The church is quiet. Only a handful of parishioners wait in line to partake of my least favorite of all the sacraments. Sebastian was right when he accused me of never going to confession.

I hang around till the last person comes out of the confessional. I open the door and kneel inside the cubicle. The partition opens. It's so dark I can barely make out Sebastian's silhouette. "Whenever you're ready," he says quietly.

"Bless me, Father, for I have sinned, but right now we need to talk about you and Abby Delgado."

"*Lucy?*" He swings back the door, flooding the tiny area with light. "What are you doing here?"

"I know you told me to leave this to the police, but something happened to Abby Delgado, and I can't let it go. I keep thinking about the last time I saw her, and...you were right. She didn't have any real friends. Even her own brother didn't like her. I feel like I owe it to her to find out the truth."

He silently walks to the front of the church, where he sits in the first pew. I follow and sit next to him.

"Does this have anything to do with...you know, your ability to tell when someone's lying?"

"Sort of. But not really. I mean, yeah, there's that, but I have this niggling sense that her death wasn't just the case of a simple heart attack. There are too many weird things surrounding it all."

"I think you're right," he says softly.

I sigh in relief. Finally! "So, are you going to tell me everything you know?"

"It's not much, but yeah, I'll tell you what I can." He looks up at the large wooden crucifix looming over the altar, then gazes back at me. "A few days before she died, Abby came to me with some concerns about a parishioner here at the church."

"Let me guess? Phoebe Van Cleave?"

He nods.

"I didn't know Phoebe was Catholic."

"Lapsed, but still a registered parishioner."

"Okay. So Phoebe was who Abby wanted you to do the exorcism on, right?"

The corner of his mouth twitches up in a very un-Sebastian like way. "No. Phoebe wasn't her intended...victim."

I cross my arms over my chest. "Maybe you should start at the beginning."

I DRIVE TO THE LIBRARY, and it's perfect timing because Will is locking up for the day. "I was wondering when you were going to show up," he says.

"Does that mean you had a chance to talk to Brittany about the keys to the rec center?"

"She said she'd think about it."

"Really?" I have to admit, I'm surprised. I figured Brittany would have the vapors at the idea of using her key in some illicit fashion. "I guess that's better than a flat-out no."

Will adjusts his backpack over his shoulder. "I rode my bike here. Want to meet me back at my house, and we can make dinner?" When I hesitate, he turns to study my face. "What?"

"What do you mean what?"

"You look like you just won the lottery."

"I have some new intel on the case."

Will moans. "You're going to be the death of me, Lucy. Between this séance and running around confronting strange men with shotguns—"

"Shut up and get in my car. We can have dinner at my place. Sarah made some of her excellent mac and cheese. I'll fill you on in everything on the ride over."

He secures his bike on the rear rack of my car. I barely wait till he's buckled into his seat before I start. "Abby wanted Sebastian to perform an exorcism on Paco."

"The *dog*?"

"Yep, and there's a whole lot more." I put my car in drive and head to The Bistro. "According to Sebastian, Abby came to him a few days before she died. Apparently, she and Phoebe Van Cleave were in this huge power struggle over their positions in the Sunshine Ghost Society."

"We already knew that."

"Yeah, but after Susan Van Dyke's death, the conflict escalated because both of them wanted Paco."

"The Canine Ghost Whisperer." Will struggles not to laugh.

"It's not funny. I think Phoebe might have killed Abby over Paco."

Will's smile disappears. "Seriously? What proof do you have?"

"None. For now. According to the autopsy report, Abby died of a heart attack, but hear me out. Susan Van Dyke used to host all these séances in her home, and Paco was a huge part of the show. Aurelia and Anthony—"

"The cook and the butler?"

"I know, it's all so Agatha Christie-ish, isn't it? Anyhoo, Aurelia and Anthony said that Phoebe and Abby argued about the dog. I guess they figured that whoever had Paco would have an advantage since he has special powers."

"Since they *think* he has special powers."

"A few days after Susan died, Paco was dognapped by Derrick, which you know about. He gave the dog to Abby, but now she was in a bind. Since she'd gotten the dog illegally, she couldn't very well run around town with him openly, hence her weird behavior last Friday at The Bistro."

"Okay. But how did Sebastian get involved?"

"Initially, she wanted him to do the exorcism on Paco. Abby told Sebastian that Paco bit someone, which is totally out of character, by the way. She thought maybe he accidentally picked up an evil spirit during his last séance."

"Ah, the old *the-evil-spirit-made-me-do-it* excuse?"

"Be serious."

"You want me to be serious about a dog that's possessed?"

"Pay attention. He's not possessed. Abby just thought he was."

Will blows out a breath. "How do you know it's out of character? You've only had the dog for a few days. Maybe he bites people all the time."

"Believe me, if Paco didn't bite Derrick Delgado this afternoon, then he'd only bite someone to defend himself. Or maybe to defend someone he really cared about."

I tell Will about my trip to the police department, how Cindy let me see the security footage and about my repeat run-in with Derrick. "I can't wait to find out what really happened to Abby and show up that...*Neanderthal* Texas Ranger. He practically told me that my place was in the kitchen!"

"I thought this was about getting justice for Abby Delgado."

"That too. Showing up Travis Fontaine is just for bonus points."

We pull into the parking lot behind The Bistro's kitchen. I turn in my seat to face Will. "This is what I think happened. Even though Abby was trying to hide Paco, somehow, Phoebe found out that she had him, and I think Phoebe stole the dog from Abby."

"This is one popular dog."

"Sebastian said that Abby wanted him to go to the rec center to solve a problem between her and Phoebe. She thought that Phoebe would listen to Sebastian because he's her parish priest. But when Sebastian got there, Abby told him everything was okay. Paco was with her, and she seemed happy. Since the security footage shows Abby going into the rec center without Paco, we know for sure that someone else brought the dog. I think Phoebe had the dog, brought him to the rec center and she and Abby made up. Phoebe went to leave, but then she changed her mind and hid somewhere in the building, waiting for Sebastian to come and go. After he left, she told Abby she wanted the dog back. Somehow, Abby must have fallen, and the stress of everything made her have a heart attack."

"I don't know, Lucy, that's pretty farfetched."

"Phoebe lied to me about Paco, and it wasn't just a casual lie. There was a lot of stress and anguish behind it. She's hiding something big, Will. I just know it."

"Let's say you're right about what happened between Phoebe and Abby. Then how did Derrick's fingerprints get on the doorknob? Unless he was telling the truth about being at the celebration?"

"Oh no. That was a big lie. I'm not sure how Derrick ties into all this, but he does. That's why it's so important that we do this séance. It's the only way we can get Phoebe to tell us what really went down between her and Abby."

"I feel like my brain is going to explode."

"Mac and cheese to the rescue?"

He's already out the car door. "You got it."

We go in through the back way that leads into The Bistro kitchen, only I don't have to use my key to get inside.

"You left the door unlocked?" Will snaps on the kitchen light. Everything looks in order.

"I was in such a hurry to go see Sebastian I must have forgotten to lock the door. No worries. I've never had a problem before. Besides, I have a watch dog now." Speaking of which, it's strange that Paco hasn't run to greet me. "Paco!" I yell.

I open the stainless steel industrial refrigerator door and

pull out a tub of macaroni and cheese. "We can eat it down here or take it up to my apartment. And if you're a good boy, I might even let you see *Ghost* again."

Will moans, but he's also grinning, so I know he really doesn't mind. As we climb the stairs, I turn on the lights to my apartment. "Paco, we have mac and cheese," I say, trying to bribe him out from wherever he's hiding.

I place the container on my kitchen counter and glance around my apartment. "That's weird. Where do you think he is?"

"I'll find him." Will goes into my bedroom. "Paco," he calls.

I pull two plates down from my cupboard.

"Lucy! Come here quick. In the bathroom."

The tone in Will's voice makes me drop the ceramic plates. They shatter into a thousand pieces as they hit the floor, but I don't care. I run to the bathroom.

Paco is lying on the floor, just as still as Abby was only a few days ago.

CHAPTER NINETEEN

"HE'S STILL BREATHING." Will rubs Paco's back firmly. "C'mon, boy, that's it." He looks up at me. "We need to take him to the vet. *Now.*"

I'm so shocked I can't move. But hearing Will's commanding voice propels me into action. I grab a towel off the rack and toss it to him. "Here, wrap him up in this."

Will drapes the towel around Paco and gently lifts him up into his arms. That's when we both see the open bottle of Benadryl on the floor.

"Oh my God. He must have gotten into my medication." I think I'm going to throw up.

Will looks me steadily in the eye. "Get the bottle, Lucy. We'll need to show it to the vet."

We're dashing to the car when I realize that I have no idea where to take Paco. "He doesn't have a vet...that is..."

"Call Lanie. She'll know where to take him."

Lanie directs me to an emergency vet's office. "I'll call

ahead and explain what's happened. I'll meet you there, Lucy."

An hour later, Will, Lanie and I are huddled in a small waiting room at the Gulfside Veterinary Clinic. The door opens. A woman in her forties with kind brown eyes greets us. *Dr. Julia Brooks* is monogrammed in teal over the right breast pocket of her lab coat. She searches our gazes. "Which of you is the dog's owner?"

I stand up to face the music. "That would be me."

She smiles tightly. "He's going to be all right."

A wave of relief washes over me like a tsunami. If anything had happened to Paco, I'd never forgive myself. "Thank you," I croak. "Thank you so much."

"You got him here just in the nick of time. He was too lethargic to induce vomiting, but we were able to pump his stomach. He's on IV fluids now." She pulls the empty Benadryl bottle from her lab coat pocket. "Do you know how many pills he might have ingested?"

I appreciate her professional tone, but I still wince at the unspoken implication that this is my fault. I could have sworn the pills were in my medicine cabinet, but I've been so tired lately... I must have left the bottle on the counter top. But with the cap open as well?

"There was at least half a bottle in there. Maybe twenty or so pills? I...I'm allergic to dogs with fur, so I've been taking Benadryl to keep from itching."

She pulls out a clipboard. "Now that he's stabilized, I'm going to need some more information. Does he have any allergies? How about his previous medical history?"

"I'm not sure."

"How old is he? What did he eat today?"

"I don't know how old he is. And he ate the usual. His dog food, which is something that Lanie recommended, and um, well, maybe he also had a blueberry muffin and a granola bar."

Dr. Brooks stares at me.

A trickle of sweat runs down my back.

I'm the worst dog mother ever.

"She's only had the dog a few days," Will says in my defense. He goes on to explain the situation to Dr. Brooks.

"I see." Her tone is friendlier now. "The dog looks familiar. Has he been here before?"

"I have no idea. Maybe. His name used to be Cornelius. Does that ring a bell?"

"I'd definitely remember a dog with the name Cornelius." Her forehead scrunches up like she's thinking hard. "Still, he looks really familiar."

"He's kind of famous," Lanie says. "He's a ghost whisperer. Has a huge Facebook following?"

Dr. Brooks makes a face. "*That* I would definitely remember too. Oh well, it'll come to me eventually. Is there anyone who might be able to fill in his history?"

I pull out my cell phone and redial the last number on my log, but instead of getting Anthony or Aurelia, Deborah Van Dyke answers.

I tell her what happened to Paco and reassure her that he's going to be all right.

"Oh, I don't blame you a bit for trying to calm him

down with medication. What a little beast. I have no idea why Susan took him in. He was always getting into things."

I don't bother to correct her assumption that I'd purposely given Paco the Benadryl. I'm more interested in her last statement. "You mean, he's gotten into pills before?"

"Not pills, but the dog was always getting into mischief. One time he chewed through the strap on my Louis Vuitton bag." I can hear her shudder over the line. "Thank God, I don't have to worry about that anymore. He's nothing more than a rude little mutt. My poor sister. I'm sure it was all his barking and carrying on that caused her heart attack."

"Heart attack? I thought Susan had cancer."

"She did, but it was in remission. Strangely enough, she died of a massive heart attack." For the first time, I hear empathy in Deborah's voice. "It was actually a blessing. Fast and quick. In her sleep. Susan was terribly afraid of lingering for weeks in pain. At least she was spared that."

I'm still processing this information when I glance up and see Dr. Brooks waiting patiently.

"Deborah, the vet needs Cornelius's health history. Is there any way—"

"Let me get you Aurelia. She'll know the information you need."

Aurelia gets on the line. I hand the phone over to Dr. Brooks, who asks her the same questions she asked me earlier, only Aurelia can actually answer them.

Dr. Brooks echoes Aurelia's answers for confirmation, which gives me a chance to find out more about Paco. He's about four years old, has no known allergies or significant health history, and surprisingly, Susan Van Dyke wasn't his first owner. She found him walking down the street a couple of years ago and took him in.

Dr. Brooks finishes up her conversation then hands me back the phone.

"Thank you," I say to Aurelia.

"Oh, Lucy! Poor little Cornelius. I'm just grateful that he's all right." I can hear Anthony in the background, shooting off a barrage of questions.

The next voice I hear on the line is his. "Lucy, it's Anthony here. Aurelia told me what happened. Is there anything we can do?"

"Not really, I mean, I'm just so grateful that Aurelia was able to provide a health history for the doctor."

"I don't understand. Cornelius has been naughty before, but never like this."

I gulp. "I must have left the pill bottle out by accident."

"That must be it. Aurelia had all of Susan's medication locked up tightly, so Cornelius was never tempted by them."

Talk about pouring salt over the wound.

"Susan was on a lot of meds, huh?"

"Oh yes. She was on all sorts of painkillers for her cancer. Aurelia was a wonderful nurse," he adds proudly. "She handled all of Susan's home regimen."

"Aurelia has nurse's training?"

"She was a certified nurse's assistant for ten years before she came to work for Susan as her cook. All that experience came in very handy when Susan became ill."

Dr. Brooks motions like she wants to speak to me again.

"Anthony, I need to get off the phone. Please thank Aurelia again for the information."

"Certainly. And...you'll let us know about the séance?"

"Sure."

I hang up. "Sorry," I say to Dr. Brooks.

"No problem. So, let me fill you in on the plan of care. We'll need to keep Paco for at least twenty-four hours." She glances at her wristwatch. "It's already past ten. How about you plan to pick him up Friday morning? That will give us plenty of time to make sure his labs all come back normal. Barring any complications, which I have to warn you, could still happen, we should be able to give him a clean bill of health by then."

Complications. "Okay, sure, whatever is best for Paco."

"Can I ask, what you plan to do with the dog?"

Before I can answer, Will pipes up. "I'm taking the dog."

I whip around to face him. "For sure?"

He nods.

"Oh, Will! Thank you!"

Lanie claps her hands. "Yay for a happy ending!"

My happy ending glow is ruined when I see the preliminary vet bill. Will takes the paper from my hands. "He's going to be my dog, so I'll pay for his treatment."

I snatch the paper back. "That wouldn't be fair. I'm the one who messed up by leaving the pills out."

"Luce—"

"*Please*, Will, this is all my fault. I need to do this.

Okay?" The urgency in my voice stops him from protesting again.

The door to the vet office opens. Brittany rushes in. "How's little Paco?" she asks breathlessly. "I came as soon as I heard the news."

I look at Will, who shrugs. "She called my cell while we were waiting to hear from the doctor, so I left her a text explaining why I couldn't talk."

"Is he all right?" she asks again. "I've been so worried! What happened?"

"He accidentally got into a bottle of Benadryl," Lanie says, "but he's going to be okay."

"Thank God!"

"I didn't know you were so into dogs," I say.

"Oh, it's not just dogs. I love *all* animals."

"Brittany is this year's chairperson for the annual shelter fundraiser," says Lanie. "She's doing a terrific job, by the way.

I give up. Not only is Brittany giving away her prize money to feed the poor, but she's also a modern-day St. Francis of Assisi. Let's just go ahead and give her the Nobel Peace Prize while we're at it.

"Now that the crisis is over, I'm heading out," Lanie says. "If you need anything, Lucy, just let me know."

I give Lanie a big hug. "Thank you for all your help. You've been awesome."

"No worries." She waves goodbye to Brittany and Will before heading out the door.

Which leaves the three of us alone in the waiting room.

"Lucy," says Brittany, "Will told me all about your special project."

"My special—oh, you mean the séance?"

"Shh," she admonishes me, keeping her voice low, "We don't want the whole town to find out. Will told me what you need, and after some careful deliberation, I've decided to help you."

"You're going to give me the key to the rec center?" I can hardly believe my own ears. "That's great—"

"No need to give you the key, silly. Not when I'll be there to let you in and lock up later."

"You mean—"

"There's absolutely no way I'm going to let you have all the fun!" Her brown eyes glow with excitement. "I'm going to be there too. A real honest to goodness séance," she whisper-giggles. "I can hardly wait!"

CHAPTER TWENTY

THE WAY I see it I have three choices:

A) I could cancel the séance.

B) I could go ahead with Brittany's plan and include her.

Or

C) I could kill Brittany for her key and do the séance without her.

I'm *sooooo* tempted to pick C or at least some version of it that wouldn't actually include murder. Maybe I could just steal her key. But then I'd be no better than her (let's not forget the kindergarten paintbrush incident).

If I want to find out what really happened to Abby Delgado, then I have no choice but to go with B.

After we make plans to meet up tomorrow night at the rec center, we say goodbye to Brittany. I drop Will off at his place then head back home. My apartment that I love so much feels empty and sad without Paco.

Before we left the veterinary clinic, Dr. Brooks let me see him. He was hooked up to an IV, and he looked so small and pitiful. He stared up at me with his big brown eyes, his tail wagging furiously like he was happy to see me. Obviously, he has no idea what a loser I am. At least he doesn't blame me for his current predicament, but then I'm blaming myself enough for the two of us.

After a fitful night, I wake up groggy, but with a clear plan in mind. I have to get my two suspects, Phoebe and Derrick, to let their guards down and confess to everything they know.

Phoebe won't be a problem. As head of the Sunshine Ghost Society, she'll be at the séance. But Derrick? I'm going to have to convince him to participate. Since he's threatened to have me arrested if I go near him again, it won't be easy.

It occurs to me that I might have an ally in all this. I fish out the business card that Gloria gave me and call her. We agree to meet at The Bistro after the lunch crowd has waned. I take her up to my apartment so we can have some privacy.

"What a great view," she says, looking out my living room window.

"Isn't it? I was pretty lucky to score this place."

After spending the morning on my feet, I'm exhausted, so I flop down on my couch and motion for her to join me.

"I was sorry to hear about Paco," she says. "I'm glad he's going to be all right, but it will be a huge loss for tonight."

"Yeah, I was looking forward to seeing him in action." As in, running around trying to get everyone to pet him.

"Oh, he's *very* talented."

"But you'll be able to, you know, tap into Abby's spirit?"

"With your help, I believe so." She smiles and once again I'm reminded of how much younger she is than the rest of her crowd. It occurs to me that I don't know much about Gloria. Does she work? Or does she actually make a living off of being a medium?

"Do you mind if I ask a question? How did you get involved in the ghost business?"

"It's a long story."

"I've got time if you do."

She shifts around in the couch so that she's facing me. "My father died when I was a baby, so growing up, it was just my mother and me. She was wonderful. Very caring and supportive of everything I wanted to do."

"Like what, join the circus?"

Gloria laughs. "Hardly. I enlisted in the military."

"Oh wow. That's awesome."

"It's a good way to grow up fast. I spent four years in the army and earned enough money with the GI Bill to put me through college. Unfortunately, while I was away, my mother got sick. I was able to get home in time to spend her last days together."

An intense feeling of sorrow is behind her words. I've never been able to pick up so much emotion from another person before. It makes me feel sad as well.

"I'm so sorry."

She stares out the window. "It must be quite peaceful, sitting here in the evenings after a long day of work."

"It is rather spectacular."

"Still, I imagine it's hard to get away from your job what with the restaurant just downstairs. Deliveries at all hours, that kind of thing." She blinks, then smiles at me.

"It's not too bad."

"I know you'll find this hard to believe, Lucy, but after my mother died, she started talking to me. It was such a... balm to my soul. I knew I had to help other people connect to their loved ones as well."

She's right. I am finding this hard to believe. But *she* believes it, and that's what's important.

"After she passed, I got my degree in I.T. and came out to Florida to take a job with a local company."

"You...work?"

She laughs. "I'm just like most people. I work, pay taxes, that sort of thing. I'm fortunate that at this point in my career I'm able to work from home, so it gives me an opportunity to indulge my passion."

"Ever been married? Any children?"

She heaves a big sigh. "No to both of those. I've tried online dating, but most men aren't looking for someone who spends their free time communing with the dead."

"I guess not."

She pats me on the knee. "Now, you didn't invite me over here to talk about my love life. Did you?"

"Not exactly. Here's the thing, Gloria." I start off by

explaining how the only way we're going to get inside the rec center is with Brittany's help.

"Actually, she could prove very useful besides just her willingness to provide the key. She was also present shortly after you found Abby's body, correct?"

"Yes, along with Sarah and Will."

"You should definitely invite them too. We really have no idea who Abby might have imprinted upon or who she might feel a kinship with."

The idea that Abby's ghost might be making herself at home inside Brittany makes me smile. "The more the merrier, huh?"

"In this case, yes."

"Then you don't mind if Aurelia and Anthony Fisk come as well? Anthony called me this morning. Even though Paco won't be participating, they'd still like to come."

"I have no objection to that. They're a lovely couple."

"The thing is... I really think that Abby's brother should be there too. He was Abby's closest relative, and like you said, you never know who her spirit might gravitate to."

She frowns. "I don't know why I didn't think of that earlier. Yes, please invite him."

I hate deceiving Gloria about my intentions, but it's the only way that I can get Derrick to the séance. "I'm afraid that Derrick and I got off on the wrong foot. But if you were to ask him maybe?" I hand her a slip of paper with Derrick's number.

"Of course. I'll give him a call. Like I said, the whole group is looking forward to talking to Abby again."

"Even Phoebe?" I ask, testing the waters. I wonder if Gloria suspects that Phoebe isn't as innocent in all this as she'd like everyone to think.

"Poor Phoebe. She's so insecure! Victor and I tried telling her over and over that Abby wasn't a threat to her position in the society, but she had trouble believing it. I'm sure she's not looking forward to whatever Abby has to tell her now."

Yeah, I bet.

Gloria gets up to leave. "So I'll see you tonight? Around midnight, outside the building?"

"I'll be there. And...you won't forget about calling Derrick?"

"Don't worry, Lucy. I'll make sure Derrick is there. Tonight, we'll talk to Abby. And all will be revealed."

CHAPTER TWENTY-ONE

AFTER GLORIA LEAVES, I head over to the veterinary clinic to check on Paco.

"He's doing much better," Dr. Brooks reassures me. "He's off the IV fluids, and we began introducing solid foods. Just a little chicken and rice." She hands me a pamphlet. "Here's a list of some dog food brands that I recommend. This breed is very susceptible to spinal cord problems, so you have to be careful to keep him at a healthy weight. Carrots are a wonderful treat. Most dogs really love them."

I glance at the list, noting that blueberry muffins and granola bars are definitely not included. "Thanks. I'll make sure to give this to Will."

I visit with Paco for about thirty minutes. He's back to his usual happy self, but I don't want to take him home before Dr. Brooks gives him the green light. "I'll come get you first thing in the morning," I say to him, stroking his back lightly. My throat tightens up. "And...we'll spend another night together before you go to live with Will. Okay? No worries. We'll see each other all the time. I promise."

Paco's tail stops wagging. He nudges me with his wet nose and once again I'm hit with the feeling that he knows exactly what I'm saying. I always knew I'd have to give him up eventually, and there's no one better to take him than Will, but I'm still torn up about the whole thing.

I hug him tightly and try not to let him see how wet my eyes are.

Since I'm expecting a long night, once I'm back home, I attempt to take a nap, but I'm too wired, so I go down to the kitchen to prep for tomorrow morning's breakfast. When I open the pantry, I realize that I'm almost out of flour. We're low on other essentials as well. Armandi's, our primary supplier, has never been so late with his deliveries. I call Sarah to ask if she knows anything about it, but she doesn't.

"I'll call him first thing tomorrow," Sarah says. Per Gloria's suggestion, I invite her to the séance, but she politely declines.

Will, who up to now has basically laughed at the idea, agrees to join us. "There's no way I'm letting you and Brittany do this without me."

I'm not sure what's motivating him. The opportunity to see what I predict will be the world's best acting job by yours truly or spending more time with Brittany. I have a strong feeling that it's the latter.

At exactly eleven-thirty p.m. Will's car pulls into the

parking lot. I grab my sweater and tote and head out to meet him.

Ugh.

Brittany is with him. She's dressed in black yoga pants, a sleek black turtleneck sweater, and black sneakers. It's like she just stepped off the set of *Mission Impossible.*

"I wasn't sure what to wear to a séance, but this seemed the most appropriate," she says, eyeing my outfit of jeans and a baggy maroon and gold Florida State T-shirt.

Since Brittany is in the front with Will, I get into the backseat of the car. "Thanks again, Brittany. For helping us out here."

"This is pretty exciting, isn't it? Sneaking into a building in the middle of the night. It's like we're all...friends and we're on some kind of big adventure."

Something about her tone makes me uneasy. It's just occurred to me that I never see Brittany with anyone her own age. She's always either by herself or with her mother.

I catch Will's gaze in the rearview mirror. He raises a brow at me as if to say, *see what I mean?*

Maybe Will and Sebastian are right. Maybe Brittany isn't so bad after all. The two of us will never be real friends, but it wouldn't hurt for me to be more open-minded about her.

Will parks his car a few blocks from the rec center. He hands us flashlights, and we begin the short trek.

"Isn't this fun?" Brittany whispers.

"Let's just hope no one gets in trouble here," Will mutters.

"Don't worry," I say. "I have a master plan."

We approach the building from the same side that I entered the day of the rec center celebration. "Hold on. We need to make sure the cameras don't catch us." I take out a towel from my tote and hand it to Will. "Toss this over the security camera in the corner over there."

"Why me?"

"Because you're the tallest. You're always bragging about how you're the best three-point shot maker on your basketball league. Here's a chance to prove it."

He grudgingly takes the towel, rolls it into a tight ball then tosses it high in the air. The towel falls perfectly over the camera, draping it completely.

"Yes!" Brittany looks up at Will adoringly. "That was awesome!"

"Not bad," I say, glancing at my watch. "It's T minus fifteen minutes. The rest of the gang should be here soon."

Brittany pulls out her key. "I'll go ahead and open up the room." She unlocks the door and steps inside.

"Remember, no lights," I warn.

I told everyone coming tonight to park anywhere but the rec center parking lot and to bring their own flashlights. The last thing we need is for some Good Samaritan to see the building lit up from the road and to report it to the police. Gloria said she would pass the info along to Derrick. I really hope she was able to convince him to come. Otherwise, this might all be for nothing.

Brittany and Will head into the building and I hang out

by the door. Gloria is the first to arrive. She's dressed simply and has a small bag with her.

"Were you able to get ahold of Derrick?" I ask.

"Yes, and he said he'd be here."

"What did you say to get him to come?" Not that it matters, but I'm curious.

"I told him that tonight we'd be speaking to Abby's spirit and that if there was anything he needed to say to her, then this was his chance." She shrugs. "I might have also mentioned something about how we were going to ask Abby if she wanted to leave the Sunshine Ghost Society anything in her will. Even if Abby does tell us that she wants to leave the society some money, the authorities won't honor that. But Derrick seemed very motivated to make sure nothing slowed down getting his inheritance."

"That's *brilliant*."

She smiles. "You know, Lucy, you and I could be good friends. You should think of coming to one of our meetings."

Me? A member of the Sunshine Ghost Society? The idea is ridiculous, but I don't want to insult Gloria, especially not when she's been so helpful.

"Darn. I just joined a book club. Between that and The Bistro, I won't have enough time for anything else."

"What book club is that?" asks a voice from the dark.

I whip around to find Victor and Phoebe. "Oh, hey, Victor. Betty Jean Collins told me about it. Not sure if they have a name or anything." I really hope they don't have one of those cutesy book club names likes Babes and Books or something equally goofy.

"I'm in that book club," says Victor. "Betty Jean said she asked someone new to join, but I didn't know it was you, Lucy! Have you started reading the J. W. Quicksilver thriller? I think it's his best one yet."

"Yeah, um, I haven't started, but I'm really looking forward to it."

Oh boy. I guess now I'll have to go to the book club meeting next Thursday. I'll go to one meeting then drop out gracefully, citing a work conflict or something.

"Will you be bringing muffins?" Victor asks hopefully.

"I pretty much think that's a requirement."

"Can we get this séance over with?" Phoebe asks gloomily. She brushes past me to go inside the building.

Victor makes a face like he doesn't know what's wrong with Phoebe and follows her through the door.

Aurelia and Anthony show up next.

"How is dear sweet little Cornelius?" Aurelia asks.

"The vet says I can take him home in the morning."

"Thanks again for inviting us," Anthony says. "This might be our last chance to be around like-minded people for a while."

Aurelia nods. "We'll be leaving in a few days for our cruise. Who knows when our next séance might be?"

A large bulky figure emerges from the shadows. "Okay, so I'm here," Derrick says. "Now what?"

"Mr. Delgado," Gloria says pleasantly, "I'm so glad you were able to join us."

Derrick takes one look at me and freezes. "You didn't say she was coming."

"Lucy is the one who put the séance together. Without her presence, I'm not sure we'll be able to speak to Abby."

"I thought you said *I* was the one Abby wanted to speak to."

"It's a community effort." She links her arm through his. "Now that we're all here, why don't we join the others inside?"

CHAPTER TWENTY-TWO

THE ROOM IS SMALLER than I remembered. Gloria instructs us all to sit in a circle. Since this is a Pilates classroom, there aren't any chairs, so we pull some mats from a closet and arrange them on the floor.

Gloria lights several candles and sets them in the middle of the circle, then takes her place across from me. I'm sitting cross-legged between Victor and Brittany. It's dark and eerily quiet.

"Let's all hold hands, shall we?" Gloria's voice echoes off the walls, adding to the spooky ambience, but all I can think is, thank God I'm not sitting next to Derrick because I would really hate to have to hold his nasty old hand. Plus, I have no idea if he even washes regularly. Who knows what kind of germs he could be spreading?

I gaze around the room. Phoebe avoids my eyes. Derrick glares at me, but that's okay. I expect by the end of the night he won't be looking quite so smug.

In Gloria's infamous words, *all will be revealed*.

I certainly hope so.

A few minutes go by. No one says anything.

Am I supposed to talk?

Is Gloria?

Just when I'm beginning to get antsy, Gloria begins. "Abby, dear friend, sister, and faithful colleague, we're gathered here tonight in hopes that you will speak to us from the Great Beyond. Come, Abby, be with us once more as you were in life. We beseech you to come out from the shadows and join us."

Silence.

O-kay. This is my cue to—

"Derrick?" a female voice asks hesitantly. "It's me, Abby."

Chills shoot up my spine, but not because we've made contact with Abby. It's Gloria disguising her voice, pretending to be Abby.

I don't know why I'm so disappointed in Gloria, but I am. I knew this séance was a sham, but I figured that at least she believed in it, but no. She knows *exactly* what she's doing. I can hear the lie in her fake voice.

"Abby?" Derrick asks gruffly. "Is that really you?"

"Yes, brother. It's me."

I'm surprised that Derrick is so gullible. I figured he would be a tough nut to convince. Maybe his guilty conscience is making him extra stupid.

"We've just made contact with Abby," says Gloria, using her own voice again. "Her spirit is willing to speak to us, but the connection is weak. I need everyone to keep their eyes closed and to concentrate on Abby. Those of you who were present when they discovered her mortal remains, think of that moment. Draw her spirit into yours."

Brittany squeezes my hand. Her eyes are shut tight like she's trying hard to do what Gloria wants.

"Derrick," says Gloria, using the fake Abby voice again, "I'm so glad you're here. We have a lot of unfinished business between us."

"We do?"

"I want you to know that despite our differences, I've always cared about you. I've always loved you."

"Same here, Abby." Derrick's voice trembles like he's on the verge of tears.

Gloria is good at this fake talking to the dead thing if she can bring a hardened character like Derrick Delgado to tears.

"And Phoebe?"

"Yes, Abby?" There's fear in Phoebe's voice, which can only mean one thing. Just like I've suspected this whole time, she's guilty of something.

"I forgive you."

"Oh, Abby! Thank you! Thank you so much!"

Hold on a minute.

As entertaining as all this is, it isn't going the way I intended. I'm the one who called for this séance. It's *my* spirit Abby is supposed to be linked to. Not Gloria's. I can't very well have "Abby" forgive Phoebe for something until I know what it is and how it might have caused her death.

I think back to the last time I saw *Ghost*. How did Whoopi do it again? Oh, yeah. She just jumped right in.

"Derrick," I say, trying to sound trancelike. "It's Abby again. I've decided to talk to you through Lucy McGuffin, who, as everyone knows, makes the best muffins in town. Lucy, thank you for finding my body. I didn't like being left alone on this cold hard floor for so long."

A collective gasp sweeps throughout the room.

"What...what do you want, Abby?" Derrick asks.

"I want to thank you for stealing Cornelius for me. He's such a sweet little dog. I miss him."

"Er, yeah, we already went through that when you were alive. You're welcome."

"But, Derrick, remember. Cornelius is a special dog. He knows what *really* happened."

"So?" Derrick says defensively. "What's that supposed to mean?"

Not the reaction I expected.

"Oh, Abby, I'm so sorry!" Phoebe breaks in sobbing.

Aha. Here we go.

"You should be sorry, Phoebe. This is all your fault."

"Wait," Anthony whispers loudly, "I thought Abby just forgave her."

"Maybe she changed her mind," Aurelia mutters.

"I never meant...that is, it wasn't supposed to happen this way," Phoebe says. "You're right. It's my fault. You said you forgave me. Did you mean it?"

"On one condition. You have to tell everyone what you did to me. It's the only way your soul can be saved."

Brittany clutches my hand so tight I think it's going to fall off. She doesn't really believe this, does she? I must be better at this than I thought.

"Yes, yes, I'll confess to everything. I'm so sorry, Abby, I never meant for us to get in that big fight. I was just so jealous because you had Cornelius."

"Go on. Tell everyone what happened. It's the only way I'll ever be at peace. Otherwise, I might have to...haunt you forever. You wouldn't want that, would you?"

"No, no," Phoebe says. She takes a big breath. "After Derrick took Cornelius for Abby, I couldn't stand it. I just had to have him for my own. So...that Friday evening, I broke into Abby's house and stole him for myself."

I knew it!

"Abby was furious," continues Phoebe. "Not that I blame you, Abby, not one bit."

"Tell them the rest of the story," I command. I have to admit, this is kind of fun. No wonder Gloria is so into this.

"Abby called me and said she knew I'd taken the dog. We got in a huge fight, and she threatened to sic her pyscho brother on me if I didn't return him."

"Hey!" says Derrick. "Who's calling who a psycho here?"

"Silence!" I say in my best Abby-dead voice. "I want the truth and nothing but the truth! You're leaving out the important details. Like what happened when Cornelius bit you, and we had to get Father McGuffin involved for the exorcism."

"*Bit me?*" Phoebe sounds confused. "Cornelius never

bit me, and that exorcism was *your* crazy idea."

Now I'm confused as well. If Phoebe wasn't the bite victim, then who was? Derrick?

"Forget about the bite for now. Continue."

"First, I need to know." Phoebe clears her throat. "Is it... very horrible where you are, Abby?"

"Yes," says Victor, "We need to know that you're all right."

Horrible?

Oh. I see what they're getting at.

"I'm in a wonderful place. Very quiet and lovely. And not hot at all. It's like...Florida, but in the winter. And I get to eat all the ice cream I want."

Phoebe lets out a huge sigh of relief. "Oh, Abby, I'm so happy for you!"

"Now, back to the business at hand. Everyone must know what really happened to me. For *their* sakes," I add ominously.

Phoebe nods. "So, Abby and me made a deal. Cornelius should be with the person he felt the strongest connection with. We decided to put him to the test and try to resurrect the old ghost haunting this place. Earlier Friday afternoon, I was here to help some of the Gray Flamingos with the pre-tour preparations, and I stole a key off of Gus Pappas. Abby and I agreed to meet here at midnight. I...oh, Abby, I'm so sorry. I *cheated*. I came a couple of hours early with Cornelius, and I tried to get him to commune with the ghost, but nothing happened. All he did was run around the building and bark."

So that's how Paco got in the building. That part makes sense now.

"Tell the rest," I say.

"There's not much else. Abby met me at the prescribed time. I told her that Cornelius didn't respond to me so she could have him. You were so happy, Abby. Remember? We made up."

"Yes, I remember, Phoebe."

"Then Abby told me that she'd called Father McGuffin to come and act as an intermediary between us, but since I'd decided to give her Cornelius, there wasn't any need. I was...ashamed of what I'd done, stealing the dog and being so petty about the whole thing. I didn't want Father McGuffin to find out, so I left through the back door before he got here. In the end, I confessed it all to him anyway the next day at the grand opening celebration. I just didn't want all that hanging over me." She sniffles. "I'm so sorry, Abby. It all must have been too much for you. If I'd known you were going to have a heart attack, I would have stayed. I would have done CPR. Maybe I could have saved you."

No one says anything for a few minutes.

Everything Phoebe has said is the truth.

I feel...awful making her relive all this. But at least now I know she didn't do anything to cause Abby's death.

Which leaves Derick.

"Thank you, Phoebe," I say in my Abby voice. "Derrick, it's time you told the truth now too."

"Me? But I haven't done nothin'."

"That's not exactly true, is it?"

"I already confessed to stealing the dog for you. What else do you want me to say?"

"You told the police you were at a poker game at your house till two in the morning and then you went to bed. You also told them that you were here at the opening day celebration and that's how your fingerprints got on the doorknob. We both know those are lies. Come on, brother, tell them everything. Tell them how I looked the last time you saw me."

A strained hush descends over the room.

"Oh my God..." Derrick whispers hoarsely, "it *really* is you."

Now we're getting somewhere! It's hard to hide my smile of satisfaction, but I do my best to stay in Abby mode. I pause dramatically and glance around the circle to gauge everyone's reactions. Brittany, Victor, Phoebe, and Anthony all seem riveted. Derrick, too, now.

Will knows I'm faking it, so he's avoiding my gaze. Probably because he doesn't want to laugh and give me away. Gloria catches my eye, and there's a gleam of...admiration? No, it's more like resignation because I've stolen her little show away from her and she knows there's nothing she can do about it without exposing herself.

Aurelia is looking at me oddly. As if she's seeing me for the first time. It's eerie, actually. I stare back at her and blink, trancelike, and she quickly looks away.

"Of course it's me," I say to Derrick. "Go on. Let's finish this."

I can practically hear him sweating. "After Phoebe over

there stole the dog away from Abby, my sister was pretty upset. Not that I blame her. What's the point of stealin' a dog just to have him stole out from under you? So she called me and told me all about their little arrangement. Said she didn't trust Phoebe to stick to her end of the bargain and she wanted me to come here as backup. Just in case things didn't go the way she planned."

"What?" Phoebe sputters. "Abby! You didn't trust me?"

"Didn't you just admit to cheating by coming here early that night?"

"I would never have—" She shakes her head like she can't believe it.

Oh boy. Talk about a complicated relationship. But back to Derrick and how he got his fingerprints on the door-knob. "And you did come and help me, didn't you, brother?"

"Well, golly, Abby, you know if you'd still been alive, I would have done that CPT on you. But seein' as how you were dead, there wasn't much I could do."

The silence in the room is deafening.

Did Derrick just admit to seeing Abby's dead body?

"You mean CPR?" Victor asks.

"Yeah, sure, that too. Look, I know I should have called the police, but what good would that have done? I'm sorry, Abby, I really am."

I'm stunned, but I manage to squeak out a response. "It's all right."

"Does that mean I'm still in your will?"

Just as I'm about to respond, the door to the room

crashes open. The overhead lights flood the room, causing me to blink.

"What's going on in here?" We all look up to see Travis standing in the doorway. He slowly takes in the scene.

"Officer Fontaine, is the building secure?" asks a female voice over his radio. "Do you need backup?"

Everyone starts talking at once.

Travis puts a hand up in the air, demanding silence.

He unclips the radio from his belt. "The building is secure. No backup needed. It was just a bunch of squirrels creating trouble."

Squirrels? I automatically shudder. Why did he have to bring them into the picture?

He and the dispatcher exchange a few more words, then he clips his radio back onto his belt. "I'd ask who's in charge here, but I have a pretty good idea." He turns and looks directly at me.

I swallow hard. "I can explain everything."

Phoebe looks around the now brightly lit room like she's just lost her best friend. "Abby, are you gone? Abby, please come back."

"Abby was never here," Aurelia says tightly. She stands and points a finger at me. "This one. She was faking it." The accusation in her voice makes me wince.

"Lucy!" Victor says, clearly shocked. "Is it true? Were you *faking* being Abby?"

Everyone turns to look at me, except Gloria, who can't very well throw stones here, can she? And Will, who knew my plan from the beginning. Everyone else looks at me with varying degrees of suspicion and disbelief, except for Brittany.

She crosses her arms over her chest. "Lucy would *never* lie to us like that. She's the most honest person I know. Right, Lucy?"

"Well...um—"

"You really are despicable," Aurelia sneers. "First your carelessness almost got poor Cornelius killed, and now you mock the very sanctity of the séance! What kind of person are you?"

Anthony wraps a protective arm around his wife's shoulder. "I don't know how we could have been so wrong about her."

"Okay, okay, I admit, that was me pretending to be Abby, but I did it because it was the only way to get to the truth. I really thought...that is, I just wanted to make sure there wasn't any kind of foul play behind Abby's death. I did this for her." Sort of.

Brittany looks as if I've just told her there's no Santa Claus.

"You mean you thought I killed Abby?" Phoebe looks hurt, and that's worse than any shock or disbelief.

"Not *killed* exactly." Even though it's chilly, sweat trickles down my back.

"I knew all along it wasn't Abby we was talkin' to," Derrick says. "She never fooled me one bit."

"Not true," I say. "Otherwise you would have never told everyone how you found your sister dead already."

This gets Travis's attention. "People," he says, "Listen

up. I don't know what you're all doing here, and frankly, I don't want to find out. But you're all guilty of trespassing. So if you don't want to spend the night in jail, then I suggest we break up this little campfire sing-along."

"Oh!" Brittany says, "Officer Fontaine, we weren't doing anything wrong. I promise. I have every right to be here. See?" She reaches into a secret pocket in her snug yoga pants and produces a key. "I teach a Pilates class here on Tuesday and Thursday nights."

"This is a Pilates class?" he asks incredulously.

"Not exactly," she admits.

"You all have five minutes to get out of here. Starting now." The restrained fury in his voice puts everyone into motion.

Gloria snuffs out the candles and begins putting away the mats. Victor and Phoebe woodenly follow her lead.

"We need to talk," Travis says to Derrick.

I follow Derrick over to listen to whatever Travis has to say. "Not you, Lucy," Travis says.

"But I'm the reason he admitted to finding his sister dead!"

Travis turns away to block me from the conversation, but no way am I going to miss out on this. So I hang back to listen.

"What's this about finding Abby dead?" he asks.

"You already know I took the dog," Derrick says in a whiny voice.

Travis nods curtly.

"So, I promised Abby I'd do whatever she needed to

keep him. She'd paid me two hundred bucks, and she promised me another hundred if I just showed up that night. Kind of like backup. Not that I would have done anything to that other lady."

"What other lady are we talking about?"

Derrick points to Phoebe. "That one. She wanted the dog too. So they were meeting here that night to duke it out. Abby just wanted strength in numbers, you know? But I got to playin' poker and forgot about the time. After I finished playing, I got here as fast as I could. Abby had told me the side door was going to be open. When I got inside, she was already dead." His voice falters. "I swear on my life. I would never do anything to hurt my sister."

"What time was this?" Travis asks.

"About two fifteen in slow time, I reckon."

"Why didn't you call the police the minute you found her?"

He groans. "You know why. I got a record. I didn't want anyone thinkin' the wrong thing. I swear, there wasn't nothin' I could do for her. She was stone cold dead. Besides, I knew they'd find her the next morning when they opened up the place."

Travis gives him a hard stare. "Against my better judgment, I believe you."

"So I can go now?"

"As fast as you can before I change my mind."

Derrick takes Travis's advice and hightails it out the door.

Gloria and the rest of her group brush past me without

a word.

I get it. They feel deceived.

Anthony and Aurelia stop on their way out to confront me. Anthony looks down at me coldly. "We'd appreciate it if you never call us again. Any communication regarding Cornelius's welfare can be made through Susan's attorney."

"I'm sorry. I never meant to...make anyone feel as if I was—"

"What?" Aurelia spits. "Poking fun at our beliefs?"

"No! That's not it at all."

She grabs Anthony by the hand, and they storm away.

This leaves just the four us, Brittany, Will, Travis and me, looking at one another.

"Sorry, man," Will says to Travis.

"I can't believe she talked you into this."

Will shrugs.

"But you have to admit, it worked, sort of," I say. "Now we know how Paco got into the building before Abby, and how Derrick's fingerprints got on the doorknob."

"Which in the long run, doesn't change squat," says Travis. "Abby died of a heart attack. Case closed. You got all these people riled up for nothing."

Brittany spins around to face me. "I hope you enjoyed making me look like a fool. I thought you were my *friend*. You could have told me your plan. I would have gone along with it. But instead... I even stood up for you! I have no idea why you dislike me so much, Lucy. Ever since kindergarten you've had it out for me. Well, I'm through trying." She sniffs like she's holding back tears, then runs out the door.

Will gives me a look that makes my heart break. He wants to follow her, but he doesn't want to hurt my feelings. I don't want him to have to choose between Brittany and me, so I'll choose for him.

"It's okay. Go find her. I'll get my own ride home."

"I'll make sure Miss Misdemeanor gets home safely," Travis says.

"Thanks." Before Will leaves he turns to give me the *we'll talk later* look. I can practically feel the disappointment dripping off him.

I feel awful. Everyone is mad at me. It's like the day Mrs. Jackson accused me of taking the paintbrushes. All I wanted to do was help, but now I'm suddenly the bad guy.

Travis makes that growly sound in his throat that I'm beginning to get way too familiar with. "I know I'm going to regret this, but can you tell me what in hell you thought you were going to accomplish here tonight?"

"I thought I could get to the bottom of how Abby really died, so I had Gloria and the rest of the Sunshine Ghost Society arrange a séance to bring Abby back. And it worked. Sort of."

We stand there staring at each other. It occurs to me that we're alone.

"You're dangerous, you know that?" His dragon green eyes bore into me. Right now, he feels kind of dangerous too, but in a totally delicious way.

For one crazy second, I swear Travis is going to kiss me.

Instead, he clears his throat and reaches over to turn off the lights. "C'mon. I'll take you home. I got a city to patrol."

CHAPTER TWENTY-THREE

IT'S FRIDAY MORNING. Exactly one week ago today, I was happily serving customers, talking up the big rec center celebration and thinking about my Annette Funicello costume. The biggest worry on my mind was how high to tease up my hair and perfecting my mango coconut muffin recipe.

Boy. What a difference a week makes.

In *Beach Blanket Bingo*, the bad guys get their due, the surfers win the day, and Frankie and Annette end up together. But this isn't a Hollywood sixties beach flick. It's real life, and even though it's barely been ten hours since the séance broke up, just about everyone in Whispering Bay has heard about last night's debacle.

The whole town hates me.

Well, except Betty Jean, who thinks I'm a hoot.

"I knew you were the right person to invite to join our book club!" She leans into the counter. "Everyone in the club wanted to blackball you after they heard about how you tricked Victor, but personally, I think we need your kind of spunky blood! Yep. I can't wait to hear your take on the latest book. Have you gotten to chapter fourteen yet? It's my favorite. If you know what I mean," she says with a wink.

This is another way that my life has changed. Last week, the thought of joining Betty Jean's book club would have made me giggle. Now, all I can do is humbly nod and be grateful that at least someone in town wants my company. Someone besides Sarah that is. But she's my partner, so she has to like me.

The old Lucy might have lied and told Betty Jean that she'd already read the book or fake her way through the book club discussion, but I've changed my ways. No more lies for me. From now on, I'm going to be one hundred percent honest with everyone. No matter the consequences.

"I'm sorry, I haven't had a chance to read the book yet, Betty Jean, but I promise, I will."

"Okay," she warns. "But make sure you do. I can always tell when someone hasn't read the book. Oh, and bring muffins. Lots of them."

"Sure thing." I fill her order and look up to see the next person in line.

Yikes. It's Gloria and Phoebe and Victor.

Sarah comes out from the kitchen and immediately sees my dilemma. "I'll take their orders, Lucy."

"Thanks, but I have to face the music." I turn and give

them my biggest smile. "Good morning, how can I help you?"

"Coffee and a breakfast sandwich," Phoebe says stiffly.

"Would you like a muffin with that?"

"No muffins for me. Not now and probably not ever."

My stomach sinks. "Okay. Coming right up."

Victor is equally frosty.

Gloria is a little friendlier, but not much. "We thought about going to the Morning Side Café. Their biscuits are infinitely superior to the ones here, but why should we deprive ourselves of the view?"

"Thanks... Look, I never meant to hurt anyone. For what it's worth, I'm really sorry."

They ignore my apology and take their coffees over to their table. I guess I can't blame them. In their minds, I made fun of something they truly believe. Which makes me a bully. Or worse.

"Sorry about that, Lucy," says Sarah. "Is there anything I can do?"

"Not really."

She pats my shoulder. "It'll be okay. People will get over it."

"Eventually?"

"Yeah." She smiles. "The good news is I signed all the waivers you forwarded me from The Cooking Channel. They have to pick you for *Muffin Wars*. Otherwise, why go to all the bother to come out here and film us?"

"It does sound pretty positive, doesn't it?" I don't want

to get my hopes up too much, but on the other hand, this *Muffin Wars* gig is all I have to look forward to right now.

"By the way," Sarah says, "we just got a delivery from Armandi's Supplies."

"Thank God. I was down to my last cup of flour." Which is an exaggeration, but still. The Bistro's pantry was getting pretty skimpy. "Did Tony say why he was so late with the delivery?"

"He said he came by a couple of days ago but we were closed, and you weren't here."

"Why does he insist on coming after hours all the time?"

Sarah grins. "I think he's hoping to catch you alone so he can flirt with you."

I laugh. "More like show off pictures of his thirteen grandchildren." Tony Armandi must be at least sixty. He's a total sweetheart, and his prices are the best for top quality items.

"Say, how's Paco doing?"

"I called the clinic this morning. According to the vet, he's good to go. I'm picking him up after the lunch crowd leaves."

"And it's for sure that Will is going to take him?"

I nod. "I'm going to have one last night with him then bring him over to Will's in the morning."

"Did I just hear my name?"

I turn around and see Will and Sebastian in line.

"The usual?" I ask.

They both nod.

"I'll get their food ready, Lucy. Why don't you take a break?" says Sarah.

Gratefully, I take her up on her offer. I pour myself a cup of coffee and join Will and my brother at a table as far away from the Sunshine Ghost Society as physically possible.

"Get any sleep last night?" Will asks.

"A little." I glance at my brother. "I suppose like the rest of the town you already know all about last night?"

Sebastian smiles in his kindly priest way, which means he must really feel sorry for me. "It'll blow over."

"Eventually." It seems as if that's my word of the day.

"How's Paco?" Will asks.

"Good. I'm picking him up from the clinic in a few hours. Thanks for letting me have one last night."

"He's really your dog, Lucy. I'll just be watching him for you."

"That's not really true." Boy, do I ever sound like a Debbie Downer. I do my best to smile and mean it. "So tonight's the big date with Brittany. Don't forget to put on deodorant."

Instead of laughing, Will makes a pained face. "I'm not sure tonight's going to happen. Brittany is pretty mad at me. She thinks I was in on the fake séance, which I was. I guess I can't blame her for being upset."

"But...that's all on me!"

"No worries, Luce. It's not like I ever really stood a chance with her anyway."

My eyeballs practically explode out of my sockets. "Are

you *kidding* me?" I shout. "What do you mean you never stood a chance with her? Will...you're completely *awesome*! You're brilliant and funny and kind and loyal and—"

Sebastian looks at me funny.

And Will looks...embarrassed.

I slowly gaze around. The entire place is gawking at me. My gaze lands on Sarah. Her blue eyes are filled with sympathy.

"And...your breath only stinks half the time," I end woodenly.

Will chuckles uncomfortably, but it's too late. *I've outed myself.*

Sebastian knows it. I know it.

And Will knows it too.

This is turning out to be the worst twenty-four hours of my life.

I jump up from the table. "Don't worry. I can fix it. I'll tell Brittany that last night was all on me."

"Lucy, it's okay," I hear Will say.

But I'm already halfway to the kitchen. I tear off my apron and toss it onto the counter. Sarah rushes to follow me. "I need to go," I tell her. "Right now."

"Yes, no worries. Go get Paco. Take the rest of the day off."

"Thanks," I mutter. I plan to do exactly that, but first I have to try and make things right again.

THE WHISPERING BAY CHAMBER OF COMMERCE is located on Main Street next door to Heidi's Bakery. I open the door and Ginny, the receptionist, automatically smiles. Then when she sees it's me, the smile fades.

"Oh, it's you."

Really? Does no one in Whispering Bay have a freakin' sense of humor?

"Is Brittany in?"

"May I ask what this is about?"

Enough is enough. "Tell her that as a local business owner, I need to speak to her pronto."

Ginny falters a moment.

"The Chamber of Commerce still works to promote local businesses, right? Which means you work for me."

She sighs. "She has five minutes before she has to leave for a meeting. I'll let her know you're here." She picks up her phone and almost immediately, Brittany comes out of her office.

Her auburn hair looks sleek and shiny. She's wearing a black linen shift that fits her size two frame perfectly. With every step she takes in her four-inch heels, she exudes confidence and poise. No wonder Will is crazy about her. Who wouldn't be?

"Lucy," she says stiffly, "how can I help you?"

Apparently, we're going to have to do this out here in the waiting room with Ginny as our audience.

"Look, I came over here to tell you that Will had no idea what was going down last night, but that would be a lie. He knew I was going to pretend to be Abby and he went along with it. He didn't do it to make fun of anyone or make anyone look foolish. He did it because I asked him to because he's my best friend. He's the best guy I know, Brittany. He's... everything and more. And he really really likes you. He's liked you forever. If you want to be mad at someone, then be mad at me. But Will doesn't deserve it."

Brittany's bottom lip quivers.

"And for what it's worth, I was never making fun of you. And... I'd like for us to be friends. Maybe. If that's what you want."

"Oh, Lucy!" She grabs me in a hug. "Really? I want that too!"

"So, we're good?" I'm a little dazed by how well this is going.

"Absolutely!"

I can't believe I'm about to say this. "And you'll give Will a chance?"

"Definitely. If you think he's so awesome, then he must be."

Not exactly the answer I'm looking for, but it will have to do.

"Okay, then."

"When can we have lunch?" she asks eagerly.

"Huh?"

"Lunch, silly! All best friends have lunch together." She snaps her fingers at Ginny. "Check my calendar and see what day I have free next week. Oh, Lucy, we have so much to talk about!"

We do?

Ten minutes later, I walk out the door in a daze with plans to meet my new "best friend" for lunch next Wednesday.

Lunch with Brittany on Wednesday and book club with Betty Jean on Thursday. I'm still trying to wrap my head around my new social calendar when Paco comes bounding through the clinic door to greet me. He wags his tail and jumps up and down.

The vet tech goes over Paco's discharge instructions, then I head to the front desk to face the music. It's a good thing my credit card has a healthy limit. Otherwise, I'm not sure how I'd pay the enormous bill waiting for me. The figure at the bottom of the paper makes me queasy. When I hand the receptionist my credit card, she informs me that the bill has already been charged to my card since it's on file and that she's mailed the receipt to my account.

"My account?"

She nods. "I mailed it to the address we had for the dog."

"Oh, okay, great. Thanks."

I really hope I hear from The Cooking Channel soon. That ten-thousand-dollar prize money can't come fast enough.

I put Paco in the car, and we head home. After everything that's happened, I just want a quiet night in. My cell phone buzzes. It's Will. I put him on my car speakerphone, then I take a deep breath and try to pretend that my little outburst from this morning never happened.

"Hey," I say.

"Hey, yourself."

"I went to see Brittany this afternoon."

"She told me. You didn't have to do that, Lucy."

"Yes, I did. So...everything still on for tonight?"

"Yep."

"Good."

"What about you? How are you doing?"

I glance over at Paco, who's watching me expectantly. It's like he knows what's at stake here with my answer. "I figure the town is going to have to forgive me or else find another way to get their muffin fix."

He laughs, but it sounds off.

I gulp. Have I ruined our friendship forever?

"Seriously, Cunningham, I'm fine. I have Paco sitting next to me, and we're going to order pizza and watch T.V."

"Sounds like fun. I'll swing by tomorrow morning and get him."

"Or I can drop him off. Whatever works for you."

"Sure. And, Lucy? Thanks for making things okay with Brittany."

"Anytime. You know you're like a brother to me."

CHAPTER TWENTY-FOUR

PACO and I swing by Tiny's Pizza and get the anchovy and mushroom special. Will hates anchovies, but since I'm doing pizza night solo this week, I can get whatever I want.

I take a long hot bath, open a bottle of wine and settle in on my living room sofa with Paco and my pizza. I've reheated it in the oven, so it's bubbly hot. This is another thing Will and I disagree on. He thinks nuking pizza is perfectly acceptable, but I prefer to take the extra time to heat it back up the right way (which is *always* the oven).

I flip through the channels.

I've watched just about everything on Netflix, and the Hallmark Channel has already begun it's Christmas programming, which I'm totally into, but the movie they're playing is one I've seen three times already.

I scroll back to the main channels and lo and behold, *America's Most Vicious Criminals* is starting. It's a new episode featuring all their unsolved cases, including Will's favorite, The Angel of Death. He's going to kick himself for missing this. I hit the record button on my DVR so that he can watch it later.

I wonder if Jim Fontaine knows about this special episode. I wish I had his number so I could call him. Maybe I should let Travis know so he can call his dad. Except Travis and I didn't exactly part on the best of terms the other night. So, no. Bad idea.

The opening credits begin. I love the theme music to this show. It's so wonderfully eerie that if the subject matter didn't already spook you out, the music alone would do it.

I finish off my first slice of pizza and only give Paco the teeniest bit of the leftover crust. "Just this one time," I say as he eagerly gobbles it down.

"Welcome to a special edition of *America's Most Vicious Criminals*." The male host's deep somber voice adds another layer of creep to the experience. "Tonight, we'll be revisiting cases involving our most notorious serial killers. The one thing they all have in common? They've never been caught."

Oh, I can already tell this is going to be epic.

A younger Jim Fontaine appears on my screen. "Detective Fontaine, what do you think the Angel's motive was to commit murder?" asks the show's host.

Jim rubs his jaw thoughtfully. "That's a question I've asked myself a lot over the past year, and honestly, the only thing I can come up with is that she or he thinks that what they're doing is for the victim's good. It's what I refer to as a God complex. The Angel thinks that they're helping ease a patient from their suffering, but no one has a right to take anyone's life. Not under any circumstances."

They show some pictures of the Dallas hospitals where the Angel struck.

"Our killer may or may not have been a nurse, but they definitely had enough medical knowledge to know how much morphine to use to overdose a patient, and how to administer it," Jim says.

As I'm watching, something Deborah Van Dyke said flashes through my head. She said she was grateful that her sister died quickly of a heart attack instead of lingering with the pain of cancer. It seems oddly similar to these cases. Only a morphine overdose wouldn't cause a heart attack. Would it?

And then I'm reminded of something else she said right after I told her that Abby had passed.

I had no idea Florida was so dangerous.

At the time I thought it was just a boorish observation, but now...

Both Abby and Susan died of heart attacks less than a week apart. Both women knew each other. And both women had links to Cornelius.

She was on all sorts of pain killers for her cancer. Aurelia was a wonderful nurse. She handled all of Susan's home regimen...

This was never released to the press or featured in the T.V. show, but our Angel left a note each time they struck... R.I.P...

Yes, poor lamb... She makes the sign of the cross... May

her soul rest in peace...

Rest in peace?

Could Aurelia be some sort of copycat killer?

Only Jim said that the police never revealed the R.I.P. notes, so that part doesn't jibe.

My mind is whirling with a million possibilities when my cell phone rings. It's the Gulfside Veterinary Clinic. Shouldn't they be closed by now? Then I remember it's a twenty-four-hour emergency facility.

"Hello?"

"Is this Lucy McGuffin?"

"Speaking."

"Hi Lucy, this is Emily, I'm the night receptionist at the veterinary clinic. I was just going over today's charges when I saw that we accidentally sent your receipt to another account. But no worries, your credit card number wasn't on the statement. Just your name and address and the final amount."

"Oh. That's weird."

"Yeah. I'm so sorry. This has never happened before, but since the dog was in just last week, we assumed the account was the same."

I still. "You mean, Paco was at the clinic last week?"

"Yeah, only his name wasn't Paco then. But it's definitely the same dog. Those I.D. chips don't lie."

"His former name was Cornelius."

"Mmmm, according to our records the dog was named Fido."

Fido? "Can I ask who brought the dog in?"

"The name on the account is Jane Smith."

"Let me get this straight. A woman named Jane Smith brought a dog named *Fido* into your clinic. Doesn't that sound strange to you?"

"A little," she admits.

"Can I ask you what he was brought in for?"

"Dog bite."

"He was bitten by another dog?"

"No. He bit his...well, I guess she's not his owner since you have the dog. This is all pretty confusing. It reads here that a woman by the name of Jane Smith brought the dog in last week for a rabies test. She said he'd bit her, and she wanted to make sure that he wasn't rabid. The chip I.D. said that the dog was registered to a woman named Susan Van Dyke and he was current on all his shots, so that was that. But we always open up an account for every client who comes in the door." There's a pause. "Uh-huh."

"What?"

"Whenever a dog bites a human, we're required to report it to the city, in case the dog has a history of aggression. Since the owner, er, this Jane Smith person seemed okay, we let her take the dog home, but there's always a follow up. There's a note at the bottom of the record stating that when animal control went out to the address she'd given, it didn't pan out. It was an abandoned lot."

"Did this Jane Smith pay with a credit card or a check?"

"Cash."

"Which makes her basically untraceable."

"Well, yeah."

"Do you remember what she looked like?"

"Sorry, I wasn't here. But like I said, no worries about your credit card being compromised. Oh, hold on. Dr. Brooks might remember her." In the background I hear Emily and Dr. Brooks exchange a few words.

"Lucy? This is Dr. Brooks. How is Paco doing?"

Paco is currently wolfing down a piece of pizza that he's stolen off my plate, anchovies and all, but I think I'll omit this piece of information. "He's doing great, thanks."

"Emily told me about the mix-up with the account. So sorry about that. I knew I remembered seeing Paco, but the circumstances were just so different, it didn't come to me until now."

"Did you see the person who brought him in? This Jane Smith person?"

"I remember she was pretty upset about being bitten, and the dog seemed so *hostile* toward her. He kept barking and snarling. It really worried me at first, but when we got him alone, he was the sweetest little thing. We checked him out, and he was fine. But we still had to report it to the authorities."

"What did Jane Smith look like?"

"Let's see, I'm so bad with faces. I'm much better with dogs, you know? But if my memory serves me right, she was probably in her late thirties, maybe early forties. Long blonde hair with some gray. Yes, that's it. I remember now thinking how much younger she'd look if she washed the gray out."

"Okay, thanks."

I can't get off the phone fast enough. My hands are shaking.

Holy wow.

I'd bet my spot on *Muffin Wars* that Gloria Hightower is the mysterious Jane Smith.

I think back to the morning that she came into The Bistro with Victor and Phoebe and Paco went crazy barking. I'd assumed his hostile demeanor had all been for Phoebe, but now in hindsight, I realize it must have been Gloria he was barking at.

But why on earth would Paco bite Gloria? He's the sweetest dog ever.

Except when someone he cares about is being threatened.

Could *Gloria* have done something to Susan Van Dyke to cause her heart attack?

I have to tell Travis ASAP. Except, Travis thinks I'm crazy. He's never going to take me seriously. But Jim will. I quickly put on my sneakers and grab a jacket. I might not have his phone number, but I know where he lives.

"I'm going out for a few minutes," I tell Paco. "You be a good boy and stay put. No getting into any of my medication—"

My mind jolts back to something Gloria said to me the other day while she was here.

I imagine it's hard to get away from your job what with the restaurant just downstairs. Deliveries at all hours, that kind of thing.

How does Gloria know that we get deliveries after hours?

Sarah said that Tony was here a couple of days ago to make a delivery, but that no one was home. It was the day that Paco got into the Benadryl. Could Gloria have driven by and seen the delivery truck in our parking lot? Or maybe it was just an innocent comment inspired by parking lot view from my apartment window.

Except, the only window from my apartment that looks down on the parking lot is the one in my bathroom, and Gloria was never in my bathroom. Unless...

I didn't leave the Benadryl out! I didn't leave the cap off the bottle.

I'm *not* the worst dog mother ever.

Gloria broke into my apartment (okay, so I made it really easy by leaving the back door unlocked). She then deliberately gave Paco the Benadryl and tried to make it look as if it was due to carelessness on my part.

But why?

My entire body goes cold as the pieces all fall together into a neat little pile.

The first victim was probably someone important to her. A patient or family member she cared about and didn't want to see suffer anymore, so she slipped them a little extra morphine.

I run down the stairs, grab my car keys off the rack near the kitchen door, and—

Whack!

The back of my head explodes.

The last thing I see before everything goes fuzzy is Gloria standing over me with a syringe in her hand.

CHAPTER TWENTY-FIVE

I WAKE up with a massive headache and a mouth that feels like it's stuffed with cotton.

What am I doing lying on the floor in The Bistro kitchen?

Then I remember that I have to tell Jim about Gloria Hightower. I try to get to my feet, but my hands are bound together tightly at the wrists, making it difficult. I grab the edge of the counter and slowly pull myself up.

"I was beginning to think that frying pan to the head did you in."

I whirl around. *Ugh.* Not a good idea. My stomach feels like a volcano that's about to erupt. Gloria stands just a few feet away, calmly holding a syringe in her hand.

My gaze darts to the kitchen door. I need to make a run for it. Under normal circumstances, I'm pretty confident I could outrun her, but with my hands tied and my head swirling, I'm not so sure.

Does she plan to inject me with that thing?

What's in it anyway?

"I take it you plan to overdose me with morphine? Or something that will make it look like I've had a heart attack?"

"Take a deep breath, Lucy. You're hyperventilating." Her tone is smug and condescending.

"And you're the Angel of Death."

She raises a brow. "All those fancy FBI people and Dallas detectives. None of them could figure it out. But you did. It really is too bad. I'm going to miss you. But I'm going to miss your muffins more."

As far as offhanded compliments from psychopathic killers go, I could do worse.

"Sorry to disappoint you, but I'm not going anywhere, Gloria."

"Oh, I'm afraid you are. I can't have you running around telling everyone who I am, can I? And in case you're wondering, it was potassium that I gave Susan and Abby. Too much isn't good for the heart, I'm afraid." She lifts the syringe up to the light to admire its contents. "This isn't potassium, though. You're much too young to stage a heart attack. Don't worry, Lucy, I'm not going to let you suffer. I'm not a cruel person. Just the opposite. I made sure there's enough morphine here to put you to sleep. Once you're out, I'll knock you on the head hard enough to do the trick this time. It's really shocking how Whispering Bay has become so dangerous. Someone broke into the kitchen intending to rob the place. You came down and caught them... Use your imagination. Everyone will be terribly sad, but believe it or not, life will go on without you."

The casual way she describes my murder makes my skin crawl.

"How do you get it? The morphine and the potassium? I mean, you just can't walk into a drugstore and get those."

"Didn't I tell you I was in the military? I guess what I didn't tell you was that I was a medic. I stayed in the reserves for almost a decade after getting out. Yes, ma'am, every other weekend I marched myself off to do my civic duty."

"Gee, thank you for your service."

"Your sarcasm isn't very patriotic." She shrugs. "Oh well. Where was I? The potassium was easy, but the morphine? That was a little harder to pilfer. I've had the vials for almost five years. In case I needed them, which I did. I'm pretty sure this stuff stays potent long after the expiration date. At least I hope so. For your sake." Gloria glances toward the door that leads up to my apartment. "Now, before I put you to sleep, where's Cornelius?"

A chill runs down my spine. She's not going to stop with killing me. She's going to kill Paco too. "He's not here. He's still at the veterinary clinic.

"Bull."

"It's true. You did a good job almost killing him the other night. He's still on IV fluids and medications."

She studies my face like she's trying to figure out if I'm lying or not. Good thing she doesn't have my special gift. Of all the lies I've told in the past week, this one is the most important.

"You don't have to hurt him, Gloria. He's not a threat to you." *Please, Paco. Please stay upstairs and keep quiet.* I chant this over and over in my head. I don't for one minute believe that he's any kind of ghost whisperer, but he does have a strong intuitive nature, and for some reason, he's bonded to me. *Stay upstairs, baby. Save yourself. Hide under the couch.*

"Don't look at me that way. I never meant to hurt Cornelius. He's an exceptional dog. So talented. Unfortunately, that was his downfall. The little minx saw me inject Susan with the potassium and he bit me." She raises her pants leg to show me a red bite mark about an inch above her ankle. "Thank God I didn't need to get a rabies shot. I'm afraid of needles." She laughs like this is funny.

I discreetly try to wiggle my wrists to try and loosen the slack on the rope. I have to keep her distracted so she doesn't notice what I'm doing. The large heavy frying pan staring at me from the counter is a hell of a motivation.

"You're not just a murderer, you're a crazy murderer and a *faker*. But then I've always known that. You're about as much of a medium as I am."

"I have to admit, you surprised me the other night at the séance. I had no idea you were going to pretend to be Abby. You're clever, just not clever enough. You should have stuck with trying to perfect your mango coconut muffin recipe. As for being crazy? Is it crazy to want to help people? Then guilty as charged. And I don't plan to stop either."

"What? You're going to go around killing more people?"

Her voice hardens. "Don't be so dramatic. I'm not going to kill anyone else, well, besides you. The Angel of Death retired fifteen years ago when she moved here to Whispering Bay. These days I help others by communicating with their deceased loved ones. It's been wonderfully therapeutic for me."

"What about Susan Van Dyke?"

"Susan was an anomaly. She needed my particular kind of help, and I had to give it to her.

"Just like you had to help your mother?"

"Yes. Just like that."

"So Susan *asked* you to kill her?"

"Kill is such a nasty word. I eased her into the next world. She has no idea the pain and suffering I saved her."

"And Abby? You think you helped her too?"

She sighs heavily. "Abby was an unfortunate incident. Just like you. She knew too much, and she had to go. Like I said, you're too clever. You should have let it go, Lucy. Even the police were willing to write off Abby's death. But no. You had to keep pressing, didn't you?"

My head is starting to feel better. Maybe if I keep her talking long enough, it'll stop spinning, and I can make a run for the door.

"So, Abby knew you killed Susan? Or did she figure it out after the dog bit you? That's what happened, right? Abby might not have known what you did to Susan, but she knew that Cornelius had an irrational hate for you. It was only a matter of time before someone else saw it and put two and two together."

"I know what you're doing. I watch T.V. too. This is the part of the plot where the *murderer* has the too-smart-to-let-live busybody tied up and confesses everything while the busybody tries to escape. Sorry, Lucy, but that only happens in really bad James Bond movies." She comes at me with the syringe.

"Wait!" I plead. "Will Cunningham is on his way over. He should be here any minute. Any second now. You'll never get away with this. And...you're right, Gloria. You were only trying to help people. I see that now."

The rope is beginning to loosen, but it's still too tight to allow me any real movement of my hands.

"Good try, but you'll say anything to save yourself. And Will is out on his big date with Brittany tonight."

At the look of surprise on my face, she snickers. "That's the thing about small towns. Everyone knows what everyone else is doing and when they're doing it. Poor Lucy. I've felt so bad for you. In love with your best friend and all this time, he's clueless. But he's a man. We can't expect them to be as astute as we are. I'm afraid that at this point of the night, you're probably the last thing on Will Cunningham's mind."

If I could grab that frying pan and smack the look off Gloria's face, I would.

Which isn't a bad idea...

I inch toward the frying pan. Unfortunately, it also

takes me closer to Gloria, but it's my only hope. If I run, she'll overpower me. I know that for sure now.

"You're right," I say trying to sound resigned. "Will isn't coming over here tonight. He wants Brittany. Not me."

"He has wonderful taste in books, but in women?" She shakes her head. "I'm sorry, Lucy."

The knot on the rope seems to be easing. I have to keep her talking so she doesn't realize what I'm doing.

"I know you're not a bad person, Gloria. If you were you'd have killed Cornelius after he bit you. Instead, you took him to the vet. Didn't you?"

"I had to make sure he didn't have rabies. No one even missed him! I thought he would be fine with Anthony and Aurelia and I'd never have to see him again, so I dumped him back off at the house. But then Abby convinced her dimwitted brother to steal the dog. As long as that dog is hanging around, I'll always be in jeopardy."

A movement near the doorway catches my attention.

Oh no. It's Paco.

How he came down the stairs without making noise is a miracle. Usually, his nails make that annoying click-click-click sound. It's like he purposefully snuck down the stairs. He's standing in the doorway, and he's looking at me with his soulful brown eyes. Only there's anger in them.

I know exactly what he's going to do.

Oh. My. God.

I hope it works. Or we'll both be dead.

Gloria uncaps the syringe. "It's all right, Lucy," she says

in an eerily soothing voice. "It won't hurt. In a few minutes you'll go to sleep, and it will all be—

Paco leaps from his hiding place near the door and sinks his teeth into Gloria's ankle. Vaguely, it dawns on me that it's the same ankle he bit before. *Way to go, Paco!*

"*What the—*" Gloria howls in pain. "Get off me, you horrible little beast!" The syringe drops from her hand onto the floor.

The frying pan on the counter lies between us. We both reach for it at the same time.

Only I'm faster.

I grab hold of the handle and swing it as hard as I can, hitting Gloria on the side of the head. "Take that, you crazy bitch!" At the same time, the kitchen door crashes open.

We both turn to look.

Will stands there with his mouth open.

Gloria turns to me, blinks like she's in a daze, then crumbles to the floor.

I wiggle out of the ropes around my wrists. Paco lets go of Gloria's ankle and jumps into my arms. "Good boy, Paco!"

"Lucy!" The look of disbelief on Will's face is almost funny. "What in God's name—what the hell happened here?"

I point to Gloria's limp body lying on the floor. "Gloria Hightower is the Angel of Death. She killed Susan Van Dyke and Abby Delgado."

CHAPTER TWENTY-SIX

SARAH MAKES another pot of coffee while I struggle to balance a bag of melting frozen peas over the lump on my head. I'm sitting on a chair in The Bistro dining area with my feet propped up while Sebastian scolds me. "Why didn't you call Travis the second you realized who Gloria was?" he demands.

"Well if I'd known a crazed serial killer was waiting for me down in the kitchen I would have."

"Ever heard of locking your door?"

"I lock my door." At least I do now. Ever since the night I came home to find Paco half unconscious, I've been careful to double check. I doubt I'll ever forget again. "I can't help it if Gloria knows how to pick a lock."

Will hands me a fresh bag of ice to replace the bag of peas. "Go easy on her, Sebastian. She's had a rough night."

I'll say.

After Will came bursting through the kitchen, he called 911. Travis and Rusty arrived within minutes and took Gloria down to police headquarters. An ambulance came too. The EMTs insisted on taking me to the hospital in Panama City. After they checked me out head to toe, they discharged me with precautions.

The first thing Will did when we got back was to call Sarah and tell her what happened. Sarah's husband, Luke, called his sister Mimi, the mayor, and despite the late-night hour, within thirty minutes half of Whispering Bay either dropped by to check on me or called. Which is really flattering, except I'm not sure whether it's to see if I'm okay, or if they're just worried they might not get their muffins this morning.

"You're right," Sebastian says. "I'm sorry, Lucy. I'm just really thankful that you're all right. But promise me you'll never do this again."

"Do what? Provoke a crazy killer into coming after me? Okay, I promise."

Paco barks happily. I kiss him on the nose. "Good boy. You saved my life."

"Thank God for the dog," says Sarah.

"He's a special one, all right." I look at Will. "Sorry, but there's no way I can give him up."

Will doesn't look surprised. "What are you going to do about your allergy?"

"I'm sure Dr. Nate can help me with that." I ruffle the top of Paco's head. "What do you say? Want to stay with me?"

He barks again like he approves, and we all laugh. I swear that dog can understand everything going on around him. How else did he know that I needed him? He might not be a ghost whisperer, but he's definitely a hero.

Sarah brings us all coffee. "I just can't believe it. All this time, Gloria Hightower was a killer. And she seemed so normal!" She glances over at Victor and Phoebe, who are talking to Viola, and lowers her voice. "Well, except for the ghost stuff."

Phoebe picks up on the first part of the conversation. "I always knew there was something off about her."

Victor nods eagerly. "Me too. I never did trust her. No sirree."

Considering that Gloria has been part of their ghost society for the past fifteen years, you'd think they'd have spoken up a little earlier.

Everyone starts trying to one-up each other with their most suspicious Gloria stories. Will goes off to the kitchen. I quietly follow him.

"Hey, I haven't had a chance to thank you."

"For what?"

"For showing up in the nick of time."

"I didn't do anything. Except call the cops, and you could have done that all on your own. If anything had happened to you..." He reaches out and grabs me in a fierce hug.

"Listen," I say stroking his back. "I'm okay. Really."

He breaks off the hug, but I can tell he's still shaken by

tonight's events. I am too, but I'm trying hard to keep it all together.

"What were you doing here anyway? How was your date with Brittany?"

"The evening ended early," he says meaningfully.

"Oh?"

"Brittany is great. We just...didn't have a lot to talk about."

My heart starts thumping wildly. "Maybe the next date will go better."

He rakes a hand through his hair. "Lucy, about what you said this morning—"

The kitchen door opens. "Hey," says Sarah. "Travis is here, and he has big news."

Will and I look at one another. The ER doctor told me that someone needed to stay the night with me to make sure I didn't develop a concussion. If I ask Will, he'll do it. We can stay up and watch reruns of *America's Most Vicious Criminals* and eat cold pizza and maybe he'll tell me what he was about to say before Sarah interrupted us.

Travis is surrounded by people, all of whom are showering him with questions about Gloria, including Brittany. She takes one look at me and hugs me almost as tightly as Will just did. "Lucy! Daddy just heard the news from one of the city councilmen, so of course, I had to rush right over here. Are you all right? Oh my God! I can't believe it. Gloria killed Abby?"

I sigh wearily. "Yep." I appreciate everyone's concern,

but I'm getting tired of telling the story over and over. I glance at Travis. "So, what's the news?"

Travis puts his hands up to get the room's attention. "Everyone, simmer down. Gloria Hightower confessed tonight to killing over ten people in Dallas, as well as Susan Van Dyke and Abby Delgado. She's going to be charged here in Florida, but I'm sure the Texas authorities are going to want to have their share of her too."

Everyone starts talking again.

Travis catches my gaze and tilts his head to indicate I follow him. We manage to find a semi-quiet corner of the restaurant. "How's your head?"

"A little sore but still the same Lucy," I joke.

"I don't know if that's a good thing or a bad thing."

"For you? Probably a bad thing."

He fights back a grin. "I stopped by my dad's place on the way over here to tell him the good news. He's ecstatic, by the way."

"I'm glad The Angel of Death case is finally behind him."

"Thanks to you."

I raise a brow. This would be my moment to say I told you so. If I wanted to be snarky, but my head aches too much to gloat right now.

"I'm sorry, Lucy. I should have listened to you."

"Why do I get the feeling that was really hard for you to say?"

"You're about to get a two for one because I was wrong about something else too."

"Really? And what would that be?"

"I think I'm turning into a muffin man."

The deep timbre in his voice makes my girl parts stand up and pay attention.

Holy wow. I think I'm in trouble.

I mean, I love Will. I always have. But I can't deny that there's an attraction here with Travis.

He clears his throat. "By the way, my dad told me to give you a message. He said to tell you that he believes you. Any idea what he means by that?"

I smile. "Yep."

"Care to share it with me?"

"Nope."

He frowns.

"Oh, Lucy!" Brittany shoves Travis off to the side. She's holding a fresh ice bag. "Sarah just told me that you might develop a concussion and that someone needs to spend the night to wake you up every hour to make sure you're okay. I *insist* that you let me do it."

"Really, that's okay. I—"

"Lucy," she says sternly. "No way am I going to let you spend the night all alone. Besides, we have so much to talk about!"

"We do?"

"Didn't you get the email from Tara at The Cooking Channel?"

"The one about wanting to come out and film the café for *Muffin Wars?*"

"*Muffin Wars*? Lucy, you silly! Did you read the whole email? And all the attachments?"

"Most of it," I admit. Well, some of it.

"You're not auditioning for *Muffin Wars* anymore. Once I knew The Cooking Channel was interested in you, I had daddy pull some strings. They're vetting you for something a whole lot better! *Battle of the Beach Eats*," she says. "Have you seen it?"

"Is that the show that spotlights a beach town and puts all the restaurants in the town in competition with one another?"

She nods eagerly "It's sooo much better than *Muffin Wars*. Lucy, this is the big time!"

"Hold on just a second. How did this happen again?"

"When I saw your audition tape, I thought, how can *all* of Whispering Bay benefit from this fabulous opportunity? Working for the Chamber of Commerce, that's just the way my mind works. And it came to me. Let's find a way for The Cooking Channel to showcase all of Whispering Bay's fabulous restaurants, and Tara suggested *Battle of the Beach Eats*. Isn't she fabulous?"

"But...so The Bistro is going to be in competition with The Harbor House and Tiny's Pizza and all the other restaurants in town? We're just a coffee house. How can we compete with your father's place?"

"Oh *that*. No worries. Each restaurant will be judged on its own merits. It's all super fair."

My head is throbbing too much for me to protest. I had a better than decent chance of winning *Muffin Wars*. But this other show? The Bistro is great, but there are some awesome restaurants here in town, and I'm not sure how we'll stack up against them.

"Is there a cash prize?" I hate to sound mercenary, but let's face it, I was really hoping for that ten grand. Besides the money I owe Will, I also have a credit card to pay off now.

"Twenty-five thousand dollars, plus the prestige of being proclaimed the Best Beach Eat in Whispering Bay. And the absolute best part? We'll be doing this *together!*" Brittany squeals. "As head of the Chamber of Commerce's PR department, this is totally my baby. I'm pretty nervous, actually. It's my first big project, but with you on board to help me, I know it will all go fabulously."

Brittany absolutely believes every word she's saying.

She hugs me again. "Who would have thought way back in kindergarten that you and I would end up being best friends?"

I inwardly moan.

It's going to be a long, long night.

THE END

THANK YOU FOR READING! If you enjoyed Lucy's antics then you won't want to miss the next book in the series, WHACK THE MOLE. Read on for a special sneak peek. If you want to know when my next book comes out and to receive exclusive for newsletter subscribers only content, please visit my website at www.mariageraci.com to sign up.

JOEY "THE WEASEL" Frizzone has been deep under-cover with one of the country's largest organized crime families and the time has come for him to testify against them. The trial isn't for a couple of weeks, and the feds need him to lay low, so they hide him in a place no one would ever think to look—a sleepy little town in Florida called Whispering Bay.

Lucy McGuffin bakes the best muffins in town. She's also a human lie detector, a talent that hasn't always been easy to live with, because, c'mon, how many times can a girl hear "It's me, not you" and keep a straight face?

Lucy's ability to sniff out a lie has given her a reputation for solving crime, so when an attempt is made on Joey's life, local police officer Travis Fontaine reluctantly seeks Lucy's help. But Lucy and Travis have a wobbly relationship. The arrogant cop thinks he's God's gift to womankind, and Lucy isn't about to become President of his fan club.

Someone in the FBI must have a big mouth because soon there are enough hitmen in town to make Whispering Bay look like a reunion site for *The Sopranos*. Then someone starts whacking the hitmen. As the body count begins to rise, Lucy realizes she has to step up to the plate. Travis needs Joey to stay alive long enough to testify, and

Lucy wants her quaint little town back, minus the mobsters.

With the help of her best friend, Will, and her rescue dog, Paco, Lucy and Travis set out to discover who's behind all the hits, because if they don't, Whispering Bay may never be the same again. *Ba-da-Bing. Ba-da-Boom.*

WHACK THE MOLE

SNEAK PEEK

The thing about being a human lie detector is that people will surprise you with the strangest fabrications at the oddest times. Take right now. Rusty Newton, one of Whispering Bay's finest, is looking straight at me, and he's just told me a whopper.

I shift my weight from foot to foot. I've been standing behind this counter for over three hours without a break. It's the busiest morning we've had all week. And it's been a record-breaking week here at The Bistro by the Beach, the café I own along with my partner, Sarah Powers. Probably because I've become a bit of a celebrity. A small-town celebrity to be sure, but when you're responsible for nabbing one of America's most sought-after serial killers, people want to come and gawk at you.

Not that I mind the gawking. Like I said, it's been terrific for business.

"You want how many muffins again?" I ask Rusty.

"A dozen." He pulls a piece of paper from the front pocket of his uniform shirt. Rusty Newton is in his mid-forties and has been a cop here in town forever. He's super sweet but not the brightest bulb on the force. "And five lattes, four turkey sandwiches and six of those oatmeal raisin cookies that Sarah makes."

"And this is for the crew back at the police station?"

"Yeah. Sure. Who else would I be getting such a big order for?"

Not for the Whispering Bay police department, that's for sure. For one thing, Zeke Grant, the chief-of-police, has already been in this morning for his coffee and muffin fix. And Cindy, the police department receptionist, is on a diet. She hasn't caught so much as even a whiff of one of my muffins in weeks.

But that's not what gave Rusty away.

It's the little hairs on the back of my neck. Whenever I hear a lie, they automatically start to tingle.

Being able to sniff out lies is a gift I've had ever since I can remember. A gift I never appreciated until a few days ago, when it helped me solve the murder of Abby Delgado, a prominent member of the Sunshine Ghost Society, a local club that claims to commune with the dead. But that's another story.

I punch his order into the computer. "Is this all to go?"

He grins in his goofy Rusty way. But before he can answer, another one of Whispering Bay's finest comes up to the counter. "What's to go?" asks Travis Fontaine.

Travis is the newest member of the force, and he looks

almost as yummy as one of my double chocolate chip muffins. I wish I could say it was the uniform, but it's not.

Travis is six foot three with dark blond hair and fierce green eyes. The women in town think that he looks a lot like Ryan Reynolds. He spent eight years on the Dallas police force before moving out here to live near his dad, Jim, a retired homicide detective, all of which makes Travis a good son.

He's also arrogant and the easiest person I've ever read in my life. Not because his face gives anything away. On the contrary. Travis has a poker face that could make him a bundle in Vegas. It's just that for some reason, where he's concerned, my Spidey sense is on ultra-alert.

"Rusty just put in a quite an order," I say. "Is the police department having a party?"

Travis doesn't even twitch. "No party. Just a bunch of hungry cops."

Right.

I have to admit, this little lie of theirs has me intrigued.

"It'll take a few minutes to get that order together."

"No problem." Travis leans into the counter. "So, how's your head?"

"Still a little sore, but I'll live, thanks."

My head met up with the backside of a frying pan a few days ago. I still shudder whenever I think about how close I came to being the Angel of Death's latest victim. Good thing my little dog, Paco, was there to save me.

Speaking of Paco, he has his own unique form of Spidey

sense, because he runs up to me like he knows I'm thinking about him. "Hey, little guy!"

I inherited the chihuahua terrier mix when I solved the murder of his former owner, Susan Van Dyke. His name used to be Cornelius, but that was way too stuffy, so he's Paco now. The members of the Sunshine Ghost Society think that he's a ghost whisperer. Which, of course, is silly, but like I said, he's special. It's almost like he can understand what the humans around him are saying.

I'm allergic to dogs with fur, but after all we've been through, there's no way I'm giving him up, so I'm on medication to keep from itching. It's not supposed to make me drowsy, but it still does sometimes. Still, it's a small price to pay for being able to keep him. I live in the apartment above the café, and he spends his days going up and down the stairs between our home and The Bistro's dining area. The customers love his cute antics, and Sarah finds him adorable as well.

Paco runs around to the other side of the counter to greet Travis. "Hey, boy." Travis squats down to scratch him behind the ears.

According to Lanie Miller, one of my closest friends and the manager of the Whispering Bay Animal Shelter, Travis is on the lookout for a dog. I try to imagine what kind of dog would go best with his personality. Probably a rottweiler. Or a pit bull.

Travis rises to his full height and gives Rusty a side look that makes the older cop slink away. It also makes me a little nervous. I haven't known Travis long, but like I said, I have a pretty good read on him. The two of us have been flirting off and on, but he hasn't asked me out yet.

I have a feeling that's about to change.

"Are you busy Friday night?"

Oh boy. I've been expecting this ever since he told me that he's now become a "muffin man." To most people that wouldn't mean a thing, but besides my lie detecting skills, I also make the best muffins in town. Not that I would say that. But everyone else does, and who am I to argue with them?

"Friday night is when Will and I watch *America's Most Vicious Criminals*."

Will Cunningham is my older brother Sebastian's best friend. My brother is a priest and the pastor at St. Perpetua's Catholic Church here in town. When Sebastian went away to the seminary, Will and I became best friends too.

I've been in love with Will ever since my seventh birthday party, when he saved me from a pack of rabid squirrels. We started our Friday night T.V. and pizza tradition when I moved back to town after graduating from culinary school, and I wouldn't miss it for anything in the world.

Travis and Will play in the same basketball league. The other night, they got a beer after their game. I know this because Will told me about it. I wonder if they talked about me. Nah.

"So how about tonight then?" he asks.

"How about tonight what?" I hate playing dumb, but I have no experience when it comes to fending guys off.

"How about we grab something to eat?"

"Tonight's my book club."

He spears me with a look that makes me squirm. "I guess that's better than telling me you have to wash your hair."

"No, really. I got invited to Betty Jean's book club, and I promised to bring muffins. Apparently, there's a big waiting list to join, so I didn't dare refuse."

Betty Jean Collins is a regular customer here at The Bistro and a real character. She's a prominent member of the Gray Flamingos, a local senior citizens activist group. She's also the eighty-year-old female equivalent of a hound dog. No man under the age of sixty is safe from her. Especially Travis.

At the mention of Betty Jean, Travis breaks down and grins. When he smiles like that, his eyes become even greener. He really is quite attractive. But he knows it, so that spoils it a little.

"So you're busy tonight and tomorrow. How about Saturday night?"

I try my hardest to think of a reason to turn him down. But there isn't one.

"I could maybe possibly be free Saturday night."

"What would it take to make that a definitely free?"

I'm about to answer when I hear my name.

"Lucy!"

Travis and I whip around to see Brittany Kelly rush into the café. "Oh, hi, Travis," she says demurely.

Travis smiles down at her, and her eyes go a little wide. Yeah, he has that effect on women. "Hello, Brittany."

"I hope you don't mind, but I need to speak to Lucy. It's super important."

Travis gives me a meaningful look. "We'll finish this conversation later," he says before joining Rusty at the other end of the counter.

"Hey, Brittany," I say like I'm happy to see her. Which, for once, I am. If she hadn't interrupted us, I would have said yes to Travis, which would have been a big mistake. According to Cindy, in the short time Travis has been in town, women have been showing up at police headquarters in droves, hoping to get a chance to speak to him.

I have absolutely no intention of being a member of the Travis Fontaine fan club. Plus, if Will finds out I went out with Travis, which he would because this is a small town, then it might ruin any chance I might have with him.

Am I attracted to Travis? Yes.

Am I interested in any sort of long-term relationship with him? That would be a resounding no.

"Lucy," says Brittany, "I just spoke to Tara, and she says that the film crew will be here on Saturday. I knew it would be fast, but I'm kind of freaking out here." She gazes around the café. "I mean, are you ready for that?"

"Relax, it will be all be fine."

"Fine? This is the Cooking Channel we're talking about here. We only get one chance to impress them."

Brittany Kelly and I have a weird history. We both grew

up in Whispering Bay and attended school together. Our relationship, however, got off on the wrong foot way back in kindergarten when she lied about stealing a brand-new set of paintbrushes. Being a naïve five-year-old, I told the teacher about Brittany's lie, which got me labeled as a tattletale and earned me Brittany's disdain for the next twelve years.

At least, that's how I saw the situation.

Brittany viewed things differently. Apparently, all this time she's wanted to be my friend. At least that's what she says now.

I sigh. Talk about ironic. Here I am about to reassure Whispering Bay's golden girl that all is good in her world. "Sarah and I are closing The Bistro early on Friday to make sure everything looks spic and span. If we aren't picked to be on Battle of the Beach Eats, it won't be The Bistro's fault."

About a month ago I auditioned to be on *Muffin Wars* (think *Cupcake Wars*), and I think I had an excellent chance to get on the show. The prize for winning is ten thousand dollars, and I could have really used it. When The Bistro came up for sale a few months ago, I didn't have all the money I needed for half of the down payment, so Will loaned it to me. He's pretty casual about wanting to get paid back, but I hate owing him money.

Brittany's daddy, who owns The Harbor House, Whispering Bay's fanciest restaurant, has a friend at The Cooking Channel who showed him my audition tape. He, in turn, showed it to Brittany. That's when she got her big idea to enter the entire town in another one of their shows,

Battle of the Beach Eats. As the PR person for the Whispering Bay Chamber of Commerce, Brittany says that she was just thinking of the entire town.

I should have been angry. I mean, there was a more than decent chance that if I'd gotten selected for *Muffin Wars,* I'd win the show. But I'm trying to be a good sport about the whole thing.

Battle of the Beach Eats pits all the major restaurants in a town against one another, which means if we get selected, The Bistro by the Beach will be competing with the other five places in town. The prize money is twenty-five thousand dollars and the right to be called the Best Beach Eat in town. Right now I'd really just like the twenty-five grand.

"I know I can count on you, Lucy," says Brittany cheerfully. "Say! We should do lunch again."

Brittany and I had lunch yesterday like regular "girlfriends." It wasn't as horrible as I imagined, but I don't want a repeat anytime soon either.

"Sure."

"Okay, when?"

"Um, maybe after the film crew does their thing? I think we'll both be pretty busy until then."

"Right! You're so smart, Lucy. Call me tomorrow so we can make plans!" She blows me an air kiss on her way out.

I slump against the counter. Talking to Brittany for five minutes is almost as exhausting as spending the morning serving customers.

Sarah comes out from the kitchen and hands me two big

bags. "Funny, I don't remember the police department ever placing such a big order."

Neither do I.

Rusty pays in cash, then he and Travis take the bags and leave.

"Whew," says Sarah. "I'm glad things are slowing down some." She eyes me. "Want to take a breather? You haven't sat down all morning."

Through the glass pane window, I see Rusty and Travis get into their squad car.

My Spidey sense slaps me up the side of the head. Or maybe it's residual ache from the frying pan incident. Whatever. Something tells me to follow them, and if I've learned anything in the past week, it's that I need to listen to myself.

"Do you mind if I take an early lunch break?"

"No problem. Jill and I can handle things for a bit."

"Thanks!" I grab a sweater and Paco's leash. He happily jumps into the passenger seat of my VW beetle.

Since Travis and Rusty are in a squad car, it's not hard to spot them.

I stay in the right-hand lane, three cars behind, going slowly but not too slowly because I want to keep up with them.

The Whispering Bay police station is next door to city hall, but instead of turning into the parking lot, Travis keeps on driving.

I knew they were up to something!

Paco sticks his head out the window. "Get back in," I

urge in case either Travis or Rusty are looking. The last thing I want is for one of them to spot me.

The squad car takes a right into Dolphin Isles, a new residential community of cookie-cutter homes. Whispering Bay is a coastal town of about ten thousand year long residents, mostly young families or retirees. But there's also a substantial vacation and snow bird crowd that rents homes in this subdivision.

Travis parks the squad car on the side of the road. I roll up behind a palm tree and kill the engine. I'm confident they can't see me.

Paco barks expectantly.

"Shhh," I warn. "We're trying to stay incognito."

He freezes like he understands, which is actually pretty cute.

I glance back at the squad car, but neither Rusty or Travis get out.

Could they be on some kind of a stakeout? My heart speeds up at the thought. But that makes no sense. All that food for just the two of them?

I make a mental note to buy myself a pair of binoculars when I notice a jogger coming toward them. Maybe mid-thirties, lean build, brown hair, navy blue hoodie. He slows down and approaches the squad car. Travis hands him the two bags of food through the car window, then the man takes off jogging in the opposite direction.

After a couple of minutes, Travis and Rusty drive off.

What in the world?

Without thinking, I start my engine and follow the jogger.

If you liked this sneak peek, make sure to check out the rest of the Whispering Bay Mystery series!

And if you enjoy romance, then check out my Whispering Bay Romance series!

BOOKS BY MARIA GERACI

Whispering Bay Mystery series

Beach Blanket Homicide
Whack The Mole
Murder By Muffin (coming soon!)

Whispering Bay Romance series

That Thing You Do
Then He Kissed Me
That Man Of Mine
The Best For Last
This Can't Be Love
Can't Stop The Feeling

ABOUT THE AUTHOR

Maria Geraci writes quirky, fun, romantic women's fiction and is a two time RITA® Finalist, Romance Writers of America's highest award of distinction in the romance publishing industry, as well as a finalist in the National Readers' Choice Awards and Romantic Times' American Title Contest. Her books feature strong women, dreamy heroes, lots of laughs and a little bit of heat. She lives in central Florida and is always on the lookout for the perfect key lime pie recipe (but not the kind they served on Dexter).

Made in the USA
Columbia, SC
20 March 2020

89647941R00162